510

D0672790

DO NOT REMOVE
CARDS FROM POCKET

ALLEN COUNTY PUBLIC LIBRARY

FORT WAYNE, INDIANA 46802

You may return this book to any agency, branch,
or bookmobile of the Allen County Public Library.

Another Spring

JUNE MASTERS BACHER

HARVEST HOUSE PUBLISHERS
Eugene, Oregon 97402

Scripture quotations are taken from the King James Version of the Bible.

ANOTHER SPRING

Copyright © 1988 by Harvest House Publishers
Eugene, Oregon 97402

Library of Congress Cataloging-in-Publication Data

Bacher, June Masters.
   Another spring.

      (Series III; v. 4)
      Bibliography: p.
      I. Title.
PS3552.A257A85   1988   813'.54   88-11310
ISBN 0-89081-641-7

Printed in the United States of America.

To
Shirley Hawkins
Whose Unwavering Courage
in
Conquering Adversity
Inspired Me
to Work Through My Own!

CONTENTS

For, lo, the winter is past, the rain is over
and gone;
The flowers appear on the earth; the time
of the singing of birds is come, and the voice
of the turtle is heard in our land;
The fig tree putteth forth her green figs,
and the vines with the tender grape give a good
smell. Arise, my love, my fair one, and come
away. . . .
My beloved is mine, and I am his. . . .
—Solomon's Song 2:11-16

CHAPTER 1
The Voice of the Turtle

Winter's long sleep was over. Or almost. The season seemed to be hopping out on one foot to Courtney. Of course, she had learned in her five years in the Washington Country that March was a fickle month. A time when mounds of dirty snow lingered in the ravines as if to mock the blinding whiteness of the sky-touching mountain peaks surrounding her special valley. Roads were always muddy and rutted. And, although the winds lost their bone-breaking punch, their bite could be bitter. The settlers might bring out seed saved from last year's crops or look with longing at unbroken garden plots. No, it was too early to plant.

But, magically, the sun could part the curtain of clouds to kiss the earth warmly. Then a million violets and crocuses would thrust their fragile necks upward like stars on stems and the world would rejoice. . . .

It was on such a day that Courtney (happily, Mrs. Clinton Desmond) heard the unmistakable mating call of a wild pigeon. The harbinger of spring. Valley folk considered the gentle cooing a tangible sign of resurrection. There should be renewal inside the heart as well. Why, then, was there a sense of waiting inside her own? Waiting for something she herself was unable to identify?

"I'll see you in the spring," Mother had written from San Francisco. "I'll see you in the spring," Lance's letter was like an echo when it came from New England. And then, shockingly, Vanessa's letter came stating in her usual brief, ambiguous way that she was tired of Europe. She planned to come to discuss something of utmost importance with Courtney. Something very terrible had happened. Most distressing. Most heartbreaking. And she was sure her sister would understand. Courtney did *not* understand. She did not understand at all. When had she *ever* understood Vanessa? And why would she, always Mother's favorite, be coming *here*?

Clint was at the silver mine. He had been too busy of late for her to get into family matters. If her husband were here now, she would talk about the strange feeling of inevitability. This feeling of being trapped. And he would laugh at her, hold her breathlessly close, kiss the part of her long black hair, and call her his "little madonna." Then her fears would dissipate like the misty clouds. . . .

Doc George and Cousin Bella had invited her to come along when they went to the fort to meet the train bringing medical supplies and Doc's new book, an updated physicians' reference, more comprehensive than *Paley's*. His copy was dog-eared with use since the latest immigrants came down with swamp fever, picked up somewhere along the Mississippi bottoms. When Courtney declined, Cousin Bella tempted her further by promising a stop at the dry goods store. There might be new yardage in stock since Easter was just around the corner.

"Thank you, but no. I have a few things to do," Courtney said. "Besides, you two need a little trip alone. You are still a bride, Cousin Bella."

"My, my! Thanksgiving seems a million years ago," Arabella Kennedy Lovelace said as if to cover her embarrassment. "We will be stopping—"

Doc George pinched his wife's cheek playfully, his eyes twinkling with mirth. "A million years the good woman says of her four months with me! I shall take that remark with a lick off the salt block like I did Uncle Andy

Allbright's comment that I was 'fittin' t'take care uv a body's horse maybe, seein' as how I'd done such a fair to middlin' job with his gout!"

Chuckling together, Dr. and Mrs. George Washington Lovelace turned toward the valley road. They would avoid the shortcut leading around the base of the mountain where the ground was still frozen to a depth of six feet, with slippery mud oozing over the surface.

And Courtney, putting on a long lightweight coat, but remembering her boots, turned the other direction and went looking for other signs of spring. She had some thinking to do.

* * *

"What a book my life would make," Courtney Glamora Desmond had thought time and time again.

The preface, she supposed, would hark back to the ancestral feuding between the two families making up her bloodline. The Bellevues and Glamoras had been at undeclared war for generations. When the descendants migrated to the New World from Europe, they brought along their differences which had begun in the mine fields—aristocracy versus gold. It was with disdain that Grandfather Bellevue (left penniless by a chain of misfortunes) entered into a marital agreement whereby his golden-goddess daughter, "The Lady Ana," would wed "Big Gabe," Grandfather Glamora's son. Gabriel Glamora adored his bride but failed to win her love or respect. Reluctantly, she gave him children to whom she was no more a mother than she was a wife to her husband: twin sons, Efraim and Donolar; and two daughters, Vanessa (who was as fickle, self-centered, and beautiful as her mother) and Courtney (whose dark, solemn face and sad eyes were pure Glamora, a "miner's daughter").

That she was hateful in her mother's eyes Courtney instinctively knew. But she did not know that Donolar was banished because he was "different" and an embarrassment to his mother as she moved in her circle of rich, fashionable, and uncaring friends. And so it was that Efraim, Vanessa, and Courtney never knew of his existence.

Chapter 1 of the book of her life would concern Courtney's memories of her childhood sweetheart, Lance Sterling (acceptable since his family, too, laid claim to blue blood) . . . Big Brother Efraim, whom she adored, and his promises that one day he would abandon his studies at Harvard School of Law, and the two of them would steal away together to a beautiful wilderness in the Pacific Northwest . . . and her awkwardly gentle father whose death brought an end to life as she knew it. Mother had trouble waiting until after the funeral to bundle her "Glamora side" offspring off for an indefinite stay with a distant cousin of her late husband's— Arabella Kennedy, a spinster, in a place called the Columbia Country (later Washington State).

Chapter 2 would be filled up with the bitter memories of saying good-byes, erased by meeting Clint on the train bringing a frightened, uncertain child of 16 to the Northwest he called his "Dream Country." Clint—Clinton Desmond, Arabella Kennedy's nephew on the Kennedy side—who was to change Courtney's life forever.

Chapters 3 and 4 would include the stages of conflict. One day Courtney was sure Clint loved her. The next he did not. Could Mother have made an "arrangement" similar to that of the grandfathers—an arrangement that somehow bribed Arabella Kennedy?

Fears allayed, Chapter 6 would deal with Clint's blindness. It would be a long chapter telling of his agony and hers, their heartbreaks and tested faith. And how the "family" (Efraim and Donolar) and the extended family

(Cousin Bella, Doc George, Brother Jim, Mandy, and Mrs. Rueben) had rallied 'round Clint and Courtney . . . her own temptation to return to the home of her childhood when Lance begged that her engagement be broken . . . but the glory of triumph!

And how many chapters would it take to tell of the obstacles that prevented the wedding time and time again? Of Mother's coming (after an unfortunate marriage to a man of title but not of principle who promptly did away with the Glamora fortune)? Of the unbelievable web woven by Clint's half brothers? And, at last, the storybook drama of her marriage . . . the walking-in-a-dream happiness of being the wife of the world's most wonderful man . . . and the shared sorrow of losing the child they both prayed for in its embryonic stages of development? A knot of remorse still chafed within her. . . .

No, a book would never tell it all. Life was not a book. Life had to be *lived*. Life was God's gift which could not be imitated.

* * *

Unconsciously, Courtney had turned from the Mansion-in-the-Wild toward Rambling Gate where so much of the frontier drama had unfolded. Early scenes, like evil beads, formed into a tight bracelet that clasped about her heart as if to choke away the beauty of more recent events—the beautiful ones.

Courtney sucked in her breath as she paused on the brow of the hill to look down upon the great, sprawling house—restored to its original grandeur by the new owners. How glad she was to have Robert VanKoten and his daughter, Roberta, purchase the onetime gambling casino. How glad she was to have Roberta for a friend. And how glad she was that the VanKotens had so graciously allowed Doc George and Cousin Bella to spend their honeymoon there. Somehow that wiped away some of the terrifying memories and almost expelled her feeling that Rambling Gate was yet to play a part in their lives.

That was foolish. The Desmond Brothers had been tried and convicted and were safely out of the way. The VanKotens very likely would occupy the great house soon. Undoubtedly, they would give parties now and then, which would please Mother. She and Mr. VanKoten got along famously; and it came as no surprise when Ana Bellevue Glamora Ambrose accompanied him to San Francisco and then opted not to return with him but to remain there until spring. . . .

Spring! Thought of the season brought back the feeling of waiting. And a loud rustling in the ferns along the creek below caused her heart to knot. Why did the setting disturb her?

Courtney turned quickly to go. Hurrying along, she recalled Brother Jim's pep talk from the pulpit during the recent prolonged freeze. "Soon the voice of the turtle will be heard throughout the land!" he proclaimed convincingly. Did turtles really have a voice? Right now, she envisioned a bleary-eyed monster with leathery skin watching her from its watery grave . . . waiting . . . waiting as she was waiting.

CHAPTER 2
Let There Be Guests

The air grew chill when the sun dropped behind the western mountains. Courtney quickened her steps, grateful to see smoke puffing from the towering chimneys of the Mansion.

Doc George's buggy was in the stable. And, sure enough, there was Clint's horse rolling in the pasture as if to shed its memory of the woolen saddle blanket.

"Brother Jim will be coming along, too."

The soft, childlike voice startled Courtney. Efraim's twin had a way of walking as stealthily as the Indians who passed occasionally in their trek to the fort to market beaver skins—harmless but aloof. Wars had ended, but . . .

"Donolar," Courtney breathed in relief. "You frightened me."

Donolar's agate eyes focused on her, expressionless but somehow seeking approval. "Look! Spring beauties," he said, holding out a bunch of the dainty, purple flowers. I must tell my butterflies and they will tell the bees."

The boy would have hurried away had Courtney not detained him. "Darling, there is something I want to tell you," she said, forcing a smile but hardly feeling her lips move. "We are going to have company. You remember Lance."

Donolar nodded wordlessly while Courtney pondered the question as to why she made mention of him first. Explaining their mother who had twice rejected them

17

and the sister who had never been in touch was not something she looked forward to.

"Well, he is coming—sometime this spring—and so is our mother—"

Donolar held out the flowers. "These are for you," then, dropping his eyes, "I do not remember our mother."

Courtney took the offering, burying her face among their fragrance to hide her tears. Nature, she thought sadly, was kind to her brother. Undoubtedly, it allowed the memory to fade quickly.

"And, Donolar," she said, trying to choose her words carefully, "we are to have another visitor—our sister, Vanessa—"

"*You* are my sister," Donolar said innocently. "I have a sister and a brother. Now, bees live in colonies. Yes, I must tell the butterflies."

With that, Donolar wheeled quickly and darted into the ferns like the child of the forest he was. There were times that Courtney envied her brother. He could weave a fantasyland and escape the cares of the world. Already he would be gathering daffodils to mingle with a few brave rosebuds to arrange as tonight's centerpiece at dinner. And he would be communing with the butterflies (which were sleeping and could hear his voice, he said)—making his "Isle of Innisfree" sound more real than the often-cruel world around him.

A busy breeze sucked in the cold of the mountains' snow and blew it out across the valley. Courtney shivered a little as she removed her muddy boots and set them beside the front door. She had forgotten her woolen gloves and now her fingers felt numb. It had seemed too warm to pull the hood of her coat up to protect her head. The snow had seemed innocent in its distance when she left. But snow, like March, was tricky. One day, old-timers said darkly, there could be another of "them mighty avalanches, like the one what our pa's and ma's

witnessed back when whites and injuns was a-fightin'—
ole St. Helen's Mountain's still moanin' 'bout it."

Courtney shuddered, remembering the grisly stories.
At that moment two powerful hands caught her arms,
imprisoned her from behind, and held her immobile.
"That coat is too light for this time of year," a belovedly
familiar masculine voice whispered against her ear.

Clint swung her around almost roughly. "Ouch, that
ear was cold! When am I going to be able to trust you
alone?"

"Never!" Courtney's voice was breathless as she stood
on tiptoe to kiss the tip of her husband's chin. The single
word altered his face completely. No longer grim and
near-forbidding, it wreathed in a smile, allowing the
firm, strong jaw to relax as she drowned in the clear-
water-blue depths of his eyes.

"Faker!" Courtney scoffed.

Clint kissed her soundly. When at last he lifted his
head, it was to say, "Seriously, my darling, you must take
care of yourself—remember the plans?"

The plans. Courtney buried her face in the rough wool
of his mackinaw. "The baby," she whispered. Could any
woman be happier—if the dream came true this time?
Oh, how good God was in His plans for woman's destiny.
For she was convinced that the Creator of all good things
wanted her to have the fully joyous, fulfilled life that
comes to women who love their husbands and are loved
in return. Whose love is so great that they want to extend
it . . . replenishing the earth . . . surrounding themselves with children. . . .

Getting seated for the evening meal was so formal it
bordered on the absurd. Six o'clock (and not a stroke
later). The usual flamboyant centerpiece put together by
Donolar's deft fingers. Stiff white linen draped over a
silence cloth so there would be no sound from the polished silverware. Candlelight chasing shadows into far

corners of the great room. Cousin Bella presiding from the foot of the table since, although she remained mistress of Mansion-in-the-Wild, it was proper for the master to occupy the chair at the head. After the Scripture reading and prayers, talk would flow freely.

But tonight was different. Mrs. Rueben lifted the lid from the tureen holding wild lamb's-quarters and mustard greens. Mandy set the venison roast, spiked with myrtle, in front of Doc George. As he carved in silence, the housekeeper and cook sat down. All others sat engrossed in thought, as if alone in the room. Donolar sat frightened, looking as if he awaited the verdict from a hostile jury. No poetry came from his pale lips. Courtney wondered if her news (not really new, just undiscussed) had upset him. If so, why did Clint look so preoccupied, so profoundly serious? His eyes sought hers, briefly catching and holding them, bringing up the corners of his mouth in a smile. But there remained a look of yearning—or was yearning the word? She must reassure him that whatever childhood love had been forged between her and Lance had flickered only once and then gone out like the candle of a flame caught in a draft. But the others?

How strange! Now, they all burst into conversation at once. Jed Amos was bitten by a dog today, Doc George related, and had brought a hair from the mongrel to be examined for hydrophobia. Josiah Bunker had "fallen from the wagon" so to speak and gone on one window-rattling jag of "rot gut" according to Brother Jim, who wiped his double chin with his napkin and held his plate out to Doc George for seconds. Too bad, as he had one foot in "the Land o' Goshen" while the other one dragged in sin. "Looked so hangdog—pray for the good brother's weakness."

Cousin Bella turned her attention to household matters, telling Courtney, Mrs. Rueben, and Mandy about new material she saw at the dry goods store. It would make beautiful drapes.

"Who's a-comin'?" Mandy inquired as she mumbled a polite, " 'Scuse me," and rose to fetch the chess custard pies from the sideboard.

"Strangers," Donolar answered quickly, "people from a faraway land—bad people, are they not, Courtney? Bad—"

Bad? Courtney was startled. She certainly had never thought of their mother and sister as being *bad*—just thoughtless, self-centered, and unfeeling. Unaware that all eyes had drifted to her, Courtney's dark eyes sought Donolar's. And what she saw broke her heart. She had never seen a human being so consumed with the desire to be loved.

"It will be all right, darling," she soothed as a mother soothes a feverish child. Disregarding her boarding school manners, she reached across the table to take his frail hand. And holding it, she explained again in a voice that was so calm it surprised her. It was spring, she said. Mother would be returning. Lance Sterling planned to come for a visit and to do some more painting for the VanKotens. Then, there was Vanessa—

"And the twins," Cousin Bella added, as calmly she pushed an imagined strand of her black-and-silver hair in place.

The twins! Courtney had forgotten. How old and—?

Arabella Lovelace lifted her chin. "Let there be guests."

But silence had returned to the room.

CHAPTER 3
The First to Arrive

April came in softly. One day the orchards were pink with promise (buds at "popcorn stage," the settlers declared). And the next day the valley was filled with bloom. Farmers pushed back the winter mulch to allow their fields to dry. Baby chicks were released from the coops. That was the outside scene. Inside, spring cleaning was in full swing.

Courtney loved spring. She had supposed its arrival would resolve this sense of waiting and was annoyed when it persisted. It made no sense. Especially when Clint and Cousin Bella were so understanding. Well—Clint had been a bit hesitant that first night. But now all was right between them.

"Did I imagine some hesitation on your part when I spoke of my mother, sister, and Lance's coming?" Courtney had asked as Clint helped her with the back buttons of her blouse the evening Donolar had made the announcement.

Clint's fingers were warm against her back and Courtney felt them tremble. "Did I seem to hesitate?"

"Just as you are hesitating now."

"Hold still, Mrs. Desmond. I am having trouble with this last button. Why in the world don't you ladies put buttons on the front of your clothes?"

"We have one question on the floor. You—you surely harbor no thoughts about—about my seeing Lance again?"

Clint finished with the button and lowered his head to kiss her bare shoulder. "About the same as you entertain thoughts of my association with Alexis," he said huskily. "We belong to each other, you and I."

How many years would she be married to Clint before her blood began to circulate normally? With a little gasp of love and appreciation, she whirled to snuggle in his arms.

Their heartbeats synchronized as the grandfather clock and the echoing cuckoo clock had never been willing to do. It was Clint who broke the magic silence.

"Lance Sterling is every ounce a gentleman. Alexis Worthington Villard Bellevue is not a lady. That covers that. It is your mother's coming that bothers me—and I gather that your sister is much like her. Efraim wonders what they are up to—"

"Nothing that will interfere with us—or our plans."

Clint drew her fiercely close. And, for a moment, Courtney was able to make herself believe it was true. . . .

Cousin Bella was equally reassuring. Her approach was different, of course. "I handled my late cousin's Lady Ana on countless occasions. This one should be no different except that it is complicated by some unexplained estrangement between her and Vanessa. Also, I wonder why she chose to return to the hinterlands with us commoners instead of choosing the city. Obviously Robert VanKoten, Esquire was bowled over by her charms. And I must say that she forgot to feign illness and tailored her style to match his." Arabella Lovelace shook her head until the heavy braids all but escaped the tortoiseshell combs. "I marvel at the woman's expertise—and we shall make the most of it."

"Vanessa's coming has put my head in a spin," Courtney had admitted. "Will the children be a bother?"

"This house welcomes children. Do I make myself clear?"

"Very," Courtney said and turned away to hide a blush. Dear Cousin Bella. She deserved to have her wishes granted. . . .

The rest of the family came to accept the idea. Not happily, mind you. But in a way that brought Courtney to realize that they had put two and two together long before the matter came to light. There simply were no secrets.

Doc George insisted that Courtney come along when he visited the Brian family. Annie had puerperal fever— happened sometimes at childbirth. And Courtney had a way of cheering the valley women, he said. Doc, pushing back his cloud of white hair with one hand and holding the reins in check with the other, urged the horse along at a smart clip. Even so, the rattle of the buggy wheels failed to drown out the roundelay of birdsong. Courtney inhaled the pine-scented air gratefully. It was good to be out again, although she suspected that he had an ulterior motive in having her accompany him. Cousin Bella was his usual companion since their marriage.

She was right. "You have been a good daughter. But there comes a time when offspring have to wean their parents just as parents wean their children."

"It is my duty," Courtney protested with a sinking feeling. "I must care for her."

"Gee!" The doctor reined his horse to the right as they met with another buggy. "Morning, ma'm—tell Alex I'll be by to have a look at that tooth." He reached to tip his hat which he had forgotten, then resumed talking. "We have to expect that your mother will lapse into invalid-ism when she fails to get her way. Let me look after the state of her health. And you—well, you read up on that book I gave you."

Courtney smiled. *Prenatal Care*, he meant. Less than subtle, the man was a dear.

Brother Jim was more concerned with the state of the Lady Ana's soul. All those husbands . . . well, he just didn't know . . . not exactly like the "woman at the well" but maybe a good sermon could pare down the number in the future. *If* she would bend an ear to an ex-boxer who now saw the light. Did Courtney know that her mother once referred to him as a *"rounder"*?

Courtney knew neither this fact, nor did she know the word's meaning.

The gorilla-like man, who zealously spread the Word as he understood it, frowned. "Could mean one who hangs around disreputable resorts. Or, could be a Methodist preacher who goes around a circuit—"

"Oh, I am sure my mother meant the latter. She would never be so indelicate—"

Brother Jim was not convinced, but 'twas nothing to start a ruction about. He would pray for her as hard as he prayed for the bibulous Josiah Bunker. "There's no such thing as being 'a little bit saved'!"

Courtney agreed. Mother and Vanessa grieved her.

Mrs. Rueben and Mandy were in agreement without knowing it. Mother had treated them with the disdain she reserved for all "servants," a little below the status of human beings. So Mrs. Rueben said the Lady's return was *verboten*. Mandy said, no, just plain *bad*. That Donolar child was right.

It was Donolar who concerned Courtney most. Each time she tried talking to him, his words were the same: "I hope my Lancaster rose will be in bloom."

Lancaster rose. The rose that betokened war. . . .

A note came from Ana Ambrose the day before she arrived. Consequently, it was Mr. VanKoten who met the train and brought her to the Mansion. Roberta and Efraim were busy with a homestead claim dispute and he hoped that the family did not mind. They did not. In fact, they were delighted to see the Lady Ana looking so fit—and so absolutely radiant. And Robert VanKoten was totally engrossed in the woman who obviously was the first person who could replace his dead wife. Courtney prayed that Mother would make him happy.

CHAPTER 4
When All Is Well

So quickly did everything happen that Courtney seemed unable to keep up. Mother moved into the room she had occupied previously without a murmur of complaint. That was unnatural but a great relief to the entire household. Her stay would be only "temporary," she said. That was the word she used before but in such a different way. When Ana Ambrose visited the first time (impoverished and ill, she said, absolutely *destitute*), she announced acidly that she would remain in this "wilderness" no longer than she was compelled to. And now? That she had other plans was plain to see. But she seemed in need of reassurance.

"You are welcome here, Mother—in fact," Courtney ventured, "Efraim, Donolar, and I are sure you will want to be here for Vanessa's arrival—"

"Vanessa!" Mother dropped the pearl-handled brush with which she was stroking her silvery-blonde hair. Quickly, she regained her composure. "When is she coming?"

"I am unsure, but soon—perhaps unannounced. There is something troubling her—something I thought you might know about."

"I am sure the two of you can resolve matters," Mother said in a complimentary voice, her way of dismissing the subject. "Let us talk of more pleasant things. Do you suppose the Lovelaces would invite the VanKotens here on Easter Sunday?"

Courtney sighed inwardly. "I am sure they would be glad to. Efraim will be joining us; and I am sure Roberta would appreciate an invitation."

Mother's eyes lighted. "Delightful!" she said with an inaudible clap of her slender hands—the highly buffed nails catching the morning light.

"Donolar always arranges the flowers. Mother—?"

Her mother, busy tracing a delicate line near her eye with concern, gave no indication of hearing.

Yes, Cousin Bella said later, the VanKotens would be welcome. Mandy was saving the last sugar-cured ham and there were still yams in the root cellar. Would the Lady Ana be accompanying them to church?

Courtney hoped so.

On the Saturday before Easter, Clint came home with eyes glowing, eager to pour out his good news. If Courtney had a moment to spare.

"Oh, my darling!" Courtney caught his hand and drew it to her heart as they hurried up the stairs. "I have not intended to neglect you—and I am afraid I have. Getting Mother settled—"

There, she had done it again. Quickly, Courtney shifted the subject to her husband's day.

"I have been concerned," Clint explained, letting go of her hand and fumbling with the key which led to the suite of upstairs rooms the two of them occupied since their marriage a year and a half ago. "You remember the cave-in—"

Remember? It had all but cost Clint his life!

"And the near walkout that followed?"

Courtney nodded numbly, her mind on the Bellevue Brothers who had stirred up the insurrection in an effort to force Clint to share the profits of the Kennedy Silver Mine. It made no difference that the mother they shared in common had no claim. That partial ownership was Clint's because Arabella Kennedy was his aunt. A walkout could have closed the mines. Was there trouble again? Clint had looked so concerned the evening Donolar announced about the guests. Remembering his struggle with the blindness, Courtney wondered if another failure would do him in. There had been a time when he seemed more obsessed with fear of failing than the possibility that he would be blind for life.

But he had looked happy moments ago. Courtney took his coat, hung it on a peg inside the cedar-lined closet, and turned to snuggle in his arms.

"You have good news. I can tell."

"The news I have is worth a kiss!"

Moments later, Clint explained the news to her as he hurriedly stropped his straight razor and shaved. The sentences came out piecemeal between dipping the sharply honed blade into the basin of boiling water and scraping it expertly down his lathered face.

"There was a time when I thought the vein might play out—putting men out of work—forcing men into farming who were doomed to failure—because they are *miners* just as farmers are farmers—you do understand?"

"Yes," she said softly, remembering her same concerns. She thought of Cara Laughten's husband. He knew nothing but mining. And then her heart tightened into a lump. What about Clint? The mines were his life, having been in the family for generations. Every day she praised God that He had remembered to bury treasure here for all who wished to search.

Well, Clint was explaining, now it looked as if the new vein could last forever! The men had agreed with his plan to create a crosscut near the original vein, abiding by all the rules of safety with the use of heavy posts for support and shaping some of them into a wigwam for ventilation. The vein was very rich—so rich that if there were a crop failure, the farmers could depend on the mines until they had another loan.

"I find it hard to imagine a crop failure here," Courtney said, her mind picturing the vast wheat fields that April's soft, warm rains had brought marching across the sleepy earth like a countless army of green soldiers. Why, the crop was bountiful!

"It happened in Oregon one year. There was smut—fungus—and the fields had to be put to death by fire to keep it from spreading."

"Oh Clint, it is not going to happen here. Pity my ignorance, but we are farther north—"

"Hey!" Clint wiped his face on the towel he had tied about his middle and crooked a finger. "Come here."

In his arms, the vision faded. Clint had used it only as an example, meaning that now he would be in a position to help the farmers out. This was the good news. She must put worrisome thoughts from her mind and get dressed for dinner this instant. The gray flannel dress with the white lace bertha would be a wise choice. It buttoned down the front!

Dinner was festive. Doc George was in fine form, having delivered three babies—and, oh yes, a colt to that skittish brood mare of the Amersons. Brother Jim (and one would have trouble believing that he did not know in advance) read of Joseph's promise to brethren of famine-stricken lands: "Now therefore fear ye not: I will nourish you and your little ones. . . ." A perfect passage to precede Clint's good news about the mine. Mother, wearing a pale blue gown (her color), blurred Courtney's gray and Cousin Bella's black into the woodwork. But, for once, she seemed unaware. She ate daintily of the simple fare as if it were ambrosia. The faraway smile on her delicately shaped lips said that none of the silly conversation penetrated her ears. The Easter Sunday plans undoubtedly were occupying her thoughts.

So . . . all was going well. Almost too well. Everything was shaping up beautifully. Why, Courtney wondered, did she persist in feeling apprehensive?

CHAPTER 5
On Easter Sunday

What a magnificent Easter morning! The hills were alive with birdsong. Apple trees bent their knees beneath the burden of blossoms. Wild roses, like pulse beats, wound in and out of the split-rail fences. And every hollow was filled with blue larkspur, empurpled by the rising sun.

Inside the Church-in-the-Wildwood, the air was heady with Donolar's roses in their bid to overpower the native field lilies brought in by settlers who still preferred wildflowers.

But what made it most special to Courtney was that her mother had consented to attend the sunrise service. Maybe it was her very first time to be inside a church except perhaps at her wedding (her wedding to Courtney's father was something Mother never discussed)—and Father's funeral, of course. Mother said church dogma was futile, and disturbing—confused persons arguing as to the existence of that place where souls were tormented, and whether the resurrection would be of body or spirit. But, if it would please the family, she would oblige and attend church.

"She is almost desperately eager to please." Cousin Bella's frown spoke of the concern Courtney shared.

The weathered church (larger inside than it looked on the outside) was packed. Ana Ambrose, elegant in a pale plum velvet suit and matching mushroom-shaped hat, followed the Lovelaces down the aisle, having refused an escort.

Oh Mother, like these people, Courtney's heart implored silently, as she and Clint followed.

Her mother gave no sign of liking or disliking. Oblivious to the hobnail-scarred floor and the rough pews, she looked straight ahead. It was just as well perhaps, Courtney thought, as Clint reached to take her gloved hand. Mother would see only filthy, unshaven men, hair tied back with colored twine to disguise the need of haircuts. The prospectors. The trappers. The farmers and miners. She would be equally unimpressed with the dated suits with high, stiff collars. Never would she look for the good underneath.

It would be nice, however, if Mother spoke to some of the women. Oh, how much it would mean to them. And maybe—just maybe—she would see herself as less "destitute."

"You have been such an inspiration, sweetheart," Clint had told Courtney. "Funny thing, these women slave for their men 18 hours a day without a murmur of complaint. But they miss the little things—the things from back east that made them feel beautiful. A silk handkerchief, a feathered fan, or maybe a lace shawl fringed with memories—the kind of things only the back peddlers show on their occasional rounds."

Clint had been boyishly pleased when Courtney made friends with the valley women. Her reward had been the look of pride on tired faces of those who had been prisoners of plainness, lost their self-esteem, and saw mirrors as enemies. It had been a joy to share her copy of *Godey's* and coax the women to add a ruffle here or there or accept a wisp of veil or some leftover lace.

"They've been driven out of their senses by their drab lives. Almost insane, the poor dears have magnified the dangers of wild animals, scalping Indians, and childbirth without proper care," Cousin Bella explained further. "Funny thing, my dear, I have looked after their needs—subtly, mind you, as they're most proud—but I guess I gave no thought to their self-esteem until you came."

So between her help and that of Cara Laughten's sewing machine and Roberta's always having leftover yardage from decorating. . . . Courtney smiled at their conspiracy and paid attention to the sermon, glad that their lives were brightened.

Brother Jim, wearing the cutaway suit he reserved for Easter, weddings, and funerals, welcomed the congregants with open arms, he said. Then, opening them to prove it, he came dangerously close to splitting the coat down the back as he mounted to the hand-hewn pulpit. Turning to face the audience, he adjusted the sleeves of his coat. His powerful shoulders were still drawn back uncomfortably far. But this was Easter. Not a day for wrestling Satan—even though Josiah's eyes looked suspiciously like they'd been marinated in blood and put back into their sockets. So best keep his coat and tie on, even though the tight shirt collar added color to his already ruddy face.

"Is it well with thee?" the Reverend Brother boomed.

"Yes, Lord, *yes*!" the congregation chorused.

"Then *sing*!"

Somebody sounded the pitch pipe. And the group burst into triumphant song:

> When peace like a river attendeth my way,
> When sorrows like sea billows roll;
> Whatever my lot, Thou hast taught me to say,
> "It is well, it is well with my soul . . ."

The melody seemed to linger in the pines above the church even after the song had died away. A feeling of peace descended. Brother Jim appeared almost reluctant to break the sacred silence. When he spoke, it was in awe.

"Easter is the memory of the stone rolled away."

"Yes . . . yes . . ." his listeners affirmed.

"Hope through the risen Lord . . . (*Yes!*) . . . the hal-lelujahs of the heart . . . (*Hallelujah!*)"

"It is comforting to know that Easter brings us new life—why, Doc George delivered a strapping nine-pounder this very morning to Cheyenne Peabody's missus . . . broad-shouldered, powerful-lunged, and a welcome member to tomorrow's choir, sure to be a bass singer! And it's comforting to know that life goes on beyond this life because of Christ's birth, death, and glorious resur-rection! Can you turn aside His gift? *Can* you? Don't leave this building, I beseech you, until it is well with your soul. . . ."

*   *   *

Courtney helped her mother prepare for an afternoon nap. "Would you like something to read? Luke told the Easter story beautifully."

Mother pushed the family Bible away. "I will have witch hazel pads over my eyes. We were up so early."

Disappointed, Courtney put the great Book back on the stand Donolar had made for it. Mother needed to know about love, the unselfish God-given love that Eas-ter spelled out. And in this Bible, she would have found it exemplified in the way Cousin Bella's spidery handwrit-ing recorded the family lineage.

But she supposed Mandy was right. "Ain't no way we's a-gonna *push* dat woman into heben!"

Mandy! Courtney had promised to help her color eggs for the valley children. Donolar loved hiding them along the roads and down along the creek.

Mandy was pouring liquid off the yellow oak bark. The knowledgeable cook had set the bark to soak yes-terday while Courtney made the frosting for Mandy's

George Washington cake. Now she would add alum and then the colors: vitriol blue base with a pinch of "sugar of lead" for yellow; cochineal and bruised nutgalls for red; and dabs of fustic, copperas, and madder for colors Courtney never heard of before. Dear Mandy, she must have had an ebony fairy for a mother!

"Miz Courtney, hon, duz y'all be 'spectin' sompin' big's bound on hap'nin' dis night?"

Courtney nodded and busied herself with removing eggs from the furiously boiling water in the granite kettle on top of the giant wood range. "Ah sho' duz," she whispered affectionately inside her heart.

* * *

It was a happy evening. Candlelight flickered and glowed on the polished silver and reflected becoming highlights in Ana Ambrose's spun-gold hair. At her request Courtney had piled it high with a cluster of curls on top. Donolar had picked dogwood along the lanes as he hid the eggs. This he made into pristine garlands and draped them the full length of the dining room table.

There was small talk after the devotions. Courtney savored every moment, so thankful was she to have the entire family together. It had been awhile since she had seen Efraim. Had he always looked so much like their mother? No wonder Roberta found him so appealing. And Roberta! How good to talk with her, to admire her heather-toned tweed suit, and to arrange for a long talk later. Meantime, Mr. VanKoten, with his usual charm, was telling Donolar a beautiful legend about dogwood being the wood from which the cross of Jesus was made.

Clint reached for her hand and caressed it. And then all was still. Brother Jim cleared his throat. Doc George coughed discreetly. But it was Cousin Bella who said, "Well, Mr. VanKoten?" as if she had caught him in the cookie jar.

It was then that Robert VanKoten endeared himself to Courtney forever. "Efraim, Donolar, Courtney," he said, touching his luxuriant blue-black hair ever so slightly. "I should like to ask for your mother's hand. Perhaps it sounds old-fashioned, but I believe that wedlock brings together families. I should like to have your approval— after I have presented my credentials. . . ."

Courtney already knew the story. But it was sweet of Roberta's father to repeat it. He was a native of Europe (as if his clipped English and impeccable elegance in mode of dress did not whisper of that). Schooling? Oxford. And, of course, further study of law at Harvard. Once he had practiced in Philadelphia, but he did not wish to return there. And—*ahem!*—it very well might be that he would not be remaining here. It depended on the Lady Ambrose . . . providing, of course, he had permission from the children's mother for the two of them to be married.

Courtney thought fleetingly of Vanessa. The timing seemed unfortunate. Perhaps she would be here before—

But no! Mr. VanKoten was explaining. "I have been long widowed and have been a lonely man. Not wishing to impose on my daughter, I have refrained from entertaining. And a more charming hostess I find it hard to imagine in all Eurasia. . . .

He paused uncertainly. And Dr. George Washington Lovelace took over.

"Maybe you should catch your breath so there can be a vote!"

Donolar, who was as susceptible to the man's charms as Mother, was first to say, "Yes, Mr. VanKoten, sir!"

And for the first time, Ana Ambrose smiled at her son.

CHAPTER 6
Surprises

The week following was a whirlwind. A whirlwind filled with surprises. It all began with where to have the wedding.

Courtney had hoped that her mother would feel drawn to the Church-in-the-Wildwood where, first, she and Clint had exchanged vows, and then Cousin Bella and Doc George. But Mother made it perfectly clear that she wished a very small wedding—very small and *very* private. That could be arranged, Cousin Bella assured her. The Mansion would be a perfect setting, with only the family. No, even more private, the Lady Ambrose said with a secretive smile. That was strange. Mother loved parties with hoards of admirers crowding around. Correction: hoards of the "right people." When the thought occurred to Courtney, she dismissed it as unworthy of herself. Perhaps Mother really was in love.

"I will need some proper clothes, however—a *trousseau*. Perhaps Efraim would be so kind. . . ."

But Mr. VanKoten would allow no such thing. Lady Ana had paid him the supreme compliment of accepting his proposal. As his wife, she was entitled to a wardrobe such as would fit her needs.

"I—I wonder, Mother—is it proper?" Courtney ventured.

Her mother pouted prettily. "Oh, my child, you really *are* behind the times here. I worry about you. Which reminds me to tell you that Robert—Mr. VanKoten—

insists that you are to visit us at length when we are settled in Bellevue—"

"Bellevue?" The word was a whisper. Courtney was remembering her mother's first meeting with Roberta and her father. That was the night he explained about Bellevue, Washington, and the far-distant Bellevue, France, overlooking the Seine River—built by Mme. de Pompadour, undoubtedly a relative.

"Yes," Mother said dreamily. "Now a village, it is near the VanKoten Perfumery. My future husband is a very wealthy man. He will be showering you with gifts."

I do not need gifts, Mother. I need your love—as does Donolar—just love us! But Courtney was silent.

Courtney and Roberta took the Lady Ambrose to the little shoppe where a temperamental French seamstress specialized in one-of-a-kind outfits. Roberta instructed her to spare no expense in fashioning three outfits, right for San Francisco's damp climate. There, the newly betrothed couple insisted, they would be married without fanfare. The new Mrs. VanKoten could shop before they set sail . . . in Paris they would "receive friends."

"Do you realize," Roberta said with a slight hint of tears in her voice, "that you and I are sisters now?"

Choking back tears herself, Courtney attempted a smile. "Is that so awful?"

The two of them stood watching the train taking away their parents until it was out of sight. Then Roberta turned to Courtney and reached out her arms. Courtney walked into them and they stood in wordless understanding. Roberta, tall and dignified (where once she was so ungainly), drew herself up full height.

"It is *not* awful. It is wonderful—the only thing wrong being that it makes Efraim my brother, too."

Courtney laughed. "There is more than brotherly love in his eyes. Roberta, what about Rambling Gate? I always hoped you would live there, but with your father gone—"

"I don't know. I honestly don't. Father was so mesmerized that he left no clear instructions—and certainly I do not wish to live there alone."

"No," Courtney said, shuddering inwardly.

The train gave a warning whistle as it rounded the last bend before winding its way from the valley and out of sight. The two girls turned away. Roberta was first to speak.

"You know, it's sad—I am happy, but at loose ends. And I have a strange feeling that we will never see them again."

Courtney's heart sagged within her. "I have the same feeling," she said. She thought of Donolar. And Vanessa. They would never be a family now. . . .

CHAPTER 7
A Visit to the Mines

A week passed, dusk-to-dawn workdays for Clint and his rapidly enlarging crew of miners. Clint took with him his midday meal (lunch to him but called "dinner" by the others, the evening meal being "supper"). The "hands" took their food in syrup buckets; but Mandy said them thangs would'n hold 'nuf to grease uh body's innards. So she prepared a hamper packed with fried chicken, loaves of sourdough bread, and whatever cake was left from the day before.

"Hit's uh sin t'be a-wastin', Mistah Clint. Whut y'all can't be digestin', jest give hit to de pore."

Even though there was enough in the basket to feed a regiment, it always came home empty.

Well, not quite.

Since Courtney had so little time with Clint, she took to dropping little notes on top of the red-checkered napkin covering the food. "Courtney loves Clint . . . You are my sweetheart . . . Hurry home to me . . . Until there are three of us!" Clint's responses had even more ardor when he had time to write. But all too frequently he could only put ditto marks beneath her words. They were the sunlight of her busy days.

When Mother's belongings were cleared away at last, Courtney sat down to write to Lance. He needed to know that Mr. VanKoten was no longer in the Northwest, that he should discard plans to paint for him. Seated at her desk, Courtney found herself frowning. Would Lance interpret the news as a suggestion that he not come? Maybe she should postpone the letter.

Feeling restless, she considered a walk. Then, seized by an overwhelming desire to see her husband, Courtney hiked up her skirt, ran down the stairs two at a time, and went in search of Donolar. She found him spraying roses, pausing now and then to allow a butterfly to land on his forefinger.

"Would you like to take a ride?" Courtney's voice was a conspiratory whisper. She had learned long ago that the butterflies did not like to be interrupted if they were talking.

Donolar blew gently against the wings of a giant monarch and sent it soaring on scalloped wings against the morning-blue of the sky. Yes—*yes!* The second *yes* was emphasized at mention of the Kennedy Mines as their destination. In minutes, he had Courtney's little mare, "Peaches," saddled, helped her up, and leaped astride a barebacked gelding he called "Pegasus."

"Were you happy about our mother's marriage?" Courtney asked cautiously when they were on their way.

"Mother? Don't you mean the grand lady? Yes, I was happy. I am glad that she smiled at me."

Dear, sweet Donolar. All he would ever have of their mother was a vague smile from a stranger he knew as Lady Ana.

Dust spiraled upward to warn that they were nearing the gaping holes so rich in silver. There had been a time when Courtney was a little jealous of Kennedy Mines because they demanded so much of Clint's time. Now, she understood and shared his pride in holding fast to the lifeblood of this corner of the Columbia River Valley. Enterprising ancestors with little more than a starvation-diet grubstake and hearts brimming with hope had held fast to their dream. Their dream was now Clint's. And Courtney would help him fulfill it to hand down to their children. No matter what sacrifices were demanded, she would meet them. Courageously . . . she was his wife!

The yellow dust closed in around them. Courtney's cough alerted Ahab. The company smithy dropped his bellows and ran to meet her, delight spreading the width of his round, sooty face and causing the whorls of wrinkles to spin around his tiny, blue-bead eyes. He extended a stubby-fingered hand then withdrew it to wipe it on his leather apron, causing the muscles to ripple powerfully along his hairy arms.

"Well, now, if it ain't th' bossman's missus, may th' good Lord be blessin' her majesty!" His merry eyes twinkled. "I betcha be seekin' th' likes o'him?"

"I am here to see all of you," Courtney said sincerely. She loved the faithful men who dedicated themselves to the needs of the miners. Carefully, eyes avoiding the black smudges left on her riding gloves by the smithy's hands, she looked toward the Company Store. Ahab followed her gaze and focused on Tony Bronson who was making haste to join them. Oh, no he didn't—the store's proprietor had no propriety on news!

"Th' bossman, he down in th' Glory Hole, he is. Hit 'nother this morning . . . bigger'n life . . . it's rich we be—*rich* . . . no more pins-'n-needles worryin'—no tenterhooks . . . *rich!*"

Ahab's honey-toned voice reached frightening decibels. The cords on his red neck stood out dangerously as the words tumbled out end-over-end, in the rush to tell all.

Tony Bronson covered his disappointment well. Maybe there was a morsel or so left that the blacksmith did not know. "No hogwash, it's happened Missus Courtney," the big, kind man beamed. "Not that we'd ask, mind ya, but guess what th' bossman's went 'n done! Cut us in, that's what—"

"He *did*?" Ahab's eyes no longer looked small. They dominated his face. But, lest it appear that he was not in the know, he repunctuated his words into a statement, "He did!"

Courtney was a bit baffled. "You mean allowed all to have shares? I am sure he feels you are entitled."

"Th' same. Funny thing 'bout folks. They work fer nothin' t'begin with. Then they work fer pay. Contented enough fer awhile, then boom they start t'grousin' 'bout conditions—"

"—'n either be quittin' or they be pilfering," the smithy nodded.

"Still 'n all, that Mr. Clint Desmond he's one wunderful man—ain't none other like 'im. Gotta new shipment of baling wire fer th' on-comin' wheat today. If Donolar here wants, he could be cuttin' 'n windin' fer me. Got in some hoarhound 'longside th' cracker barrel—"

Donolar and Tony Bronson turned to the log building housing emergency supplies for miners, trappers, and farmers. He had been the storekeeper for almost three generations. And there were those who said some of his merchandise had been in stock for the same length of time.

Ahab returned to his fiery forge and Courtney picked her way through the tree stumps in hopes of seeing Clint emerge from one of the dark caverns. She did not have to wait long.

Clint crawled from the newest of the mountain tunnels looking as if he had had a mud bath and forgotten the rinse. But his face glowed with welcome and his blue, blue eyes were almost purple with joy. Courtney knew the look. Victory!

"Oh darling, I heard," she said, rushing to him and reaching out her arms.

"Whoa—wait, sweetheart. I am muddy and—"

"You can do my dress no more damage than Ahab did to my hands. Oh Clint, aren't you glad to see me?"

"*Glad*," he moaned. "Glad is not the word. I'd have died if I had missed sharing this moment with you!"

And then she was in his arms, held breathlessly close, feeling the mud seep through her blouse, and not caring. Clint's mud-caked cheek was against hers, his lips on her hair, and for the moment the world dissolved.

Reluctantly, Clint unclasped her hands from the back of his head. "I have to get back, my sweet. The men are waiting for lanterns—oh well, a few stolen moments will make little difference. Come with me."

Giggling like two truant school children, they splashed their faces in the crystal stream that gurgled happily on its way to the mighty Columbia River. Then, hidden from the world in a ferny dell on its bank, they shared a quick lunch while Clint told of the richest strike yet . . . requiring new tracks for the carts . . . taking the silver from the sides first . . . regrouping . . . installing a "mortise" (whatever that was) for the "tenon" (and that?). But Courtney could listen intelligently to most of Clint's animated talk. Certainly she understood what he meant by saying that once they had been "land rich" and "money poor." Now, in a sense, it was reversed—Clint having allowed those in his aunt's employ to homestead the rich land for "cropping."

Courtney sat sucking on a wishbone, thinking of the breathtaking sight of the wheat fields she and Donolar had seen today. The temperature was just right since a warm rain and Chinook wind induced the big thaw. No more frosts now. And, like the farmers said, you could stand and watch the black-green shoots grow. Farmers were already sharpening their scythes and looking for the "temporaries," men who followed the harvest and had no desire to settle down.

"You're very wonderful, you know, giving the family men the pick of the land—and now giving shares of the mines—"

"Mr. Wonderful, that's me," Clint teased, checking his pocketwatch quickly. "Just pray that it all works out. Here, give me that wishbone!"

Courtney solemnly turned one end of the breastbone toward Clint and clung to the other. "Make your wish—and *pull*!"

"Guess what I wished," Courtney said smugly when she won the game by getting the longer piece of the broken bone.

"I *know*! And you're right—I will make a wonderful father!"

He left her then. Left her to dream—and pray.

The sky turned primrose and then heather. And still she did not move. Until behind her a horse blew softly and stealthy footsteps eased down the bank. A pair of black shiny boots stopped beside her—just inches away.

CHAPTER 8
More Than a
Chance Encounter

Even as Clint, Courtney, and Donolar rode home through the thickening twilight, Courtney heard only an occasional word. Clint's explaining the good fortune at the mines to her brother allowed her to review with pain and perplexity the encounter with Horace Bellevue.

Her first thought as, startled, her eyes traveled beyond the shiny boots, past the perfectly creased trousers and faultlessly white shirt, to meet his thin-lipped smile, was: *How do you manage to stay so well-groomed and work—if work you do?*

The question dissolved into something she could only identify as annoyance. "I have tried to make it clear," she said in a voice brittle with displeasure, "that I dislike having you approach me from behind—without a greeting or warning."

His manner infuriated her. The benign smile said he was dealing with a temperamental child. "Good afternoon, dear cousin—or should I call you 'sister' now that you and my half brother—"

"Call me neither," Courtney said as she attempted to scramble to her feet. "My name is—"

At that precise moment, the heel of her boot became ensnared in a clump of ferns and she would have fallen forward had Horace Bellevue not reached out to steady her. Before she could catch her breath and move away, Courtney had the distinct vision of his rapier glance which examined every detail of her being. She was aware, too, that he had not let go of her arms. It was

46

almost, she thought furiously when at last she found strength to wrench free, as if he had planned the moment. Certainly he was making the most of it.

"Don't rush away too fast, my dear. It would look a trifle suspicious if you went tearing out of the brush with me at your heels. It is best that we saunter along casually—just talking—"

Although she could hardly tolerate the mocking taunt, Courtney supposed he had a point. Head erect, she climbed the bank, shrugging off any offer of help.

"So to keep the conversation going, I will tell you that I have been to the city on business for Clint. Smile!"

Courtney took a deep breath and adjusted a tight smile for the benefit of a cluster of miners just ahead. This man had an exasperating way of turning every incident into an insult without doing anything she could exactly pin down. Or that she could tell Clint. Or even discuss with Cousin Bella. Put simply, he made her feel dirty with his over-familiarity.

"We should be talking, you know," he chided. "You are most uncooperative, my dear, so I will tell you why it was necessary to approach you from behind. Otherwise, I would have had to swim the creek. Then we could have met face to face as I met Roberta in town—"

"Miss VanKoten," Courtney corrected coldly.

"Ah, yes, Miss VanKoten—the very eligible young lady. Tell me," Horace Bellevue lowered his voice, "has your brother declared his intentions?"

Something inside Courtney exploded. "That is none of your business!" she hissed.

He had hit a nerve and he knew it. His laugh was that of the gloating victor. "What does Ro—Miss VanKoten—plan to do with Rambling Gate?"

"That is none of your affair either."

"Oh, but it is!" There was anger in his voice, anger which made her happy to see Donolar and Mr. Bronson coming from the door to stand on the porch of the Company Store. . . .

*   *   *

Clint reined in at the Mansion and helped Courtney from her mare. "You are very quiet. I have a feeling we need to talk—but darling, I will have to go back tonight—"

Courtney nodded. Tonight and lots of others. This was no time to discuss his half brother. But one day he must be reckoned with. Today was no chance meeting . . . but this, too, must wait.

CHAPTER 9
A Letter from Lance

May Day! Courtney remembered the childhood pleasures of pasting together paper baskets as she and Lance hid themselves in the hedge separating the formal gardens of the Glamora and Sterling homes. They must be quiet, very quiet, as they filled them with grasses and whatever wildflowers braved the sometimes-raw spring. Later, they would tiptoe from house to house to hang the flimsy handles on doorknobs, then make a quick getaway before being discovered. She smiled at the memory of how they doubled up in laughter once they were safely back in their "hedge house."

It was a beautiful memory. Why, then, did the recollection cause her melancholy? Everything she could possibly want was here: love of the most wonderful man in the world, love of a family denied her in that long-ago childhood, and all her dreams coming true. And more! Here, in Clint's "Dream Country," she had seen countless desires fulfilled to make it worthy of his name. Divinely happy herself, Courtney had taken great delight in Cousin Bella's marriage to Doc George. And, although she had some reservations regarding her mother's capacity to love, Robert VanKoten's devotion blinded him to his wife's flaws. Then there were Roberta and Efraim. The two of them just might follow suit—unless Roberta devoured him with her amber-brown eyes before he saw beyond her keen legal mind. Courtney wished Efraim would declare his love and . . . and . . . (her heart swelled, beating wildly) . . . start a family. She steeled herself against such thinking.

Think about the mines, she willed. After a catalog of catastrophes, they were graciously yielding to pick and shovel faster than the men could haul the silver to the surface. Silver ores proper. And silver as a by-product by amalgamation. Referred to as "Abraham's wealth" by Brother Jim, the precious metal meant more than a fortune to Clint. It meant livelihood for the valley in case of disaster. But disaster was an unpleasant thought, too.

Why not concentrate on the wheat? See the leggy, green stalks nodding their golden heads waiting for the most bountiful harvest ever. Gold . . . pure gold . . . and worth more than the silver.

Yes, all was going well. Maybe it was Vanessa's impending visit that concerned her. What could be so "terrible, awful" when her sister had a pair of twins?

And then Courtney recognized her melancholy, her sense of waiting, for what it was. For months her loss of the unborn child had been an unending ache. Even now, the grief reached out and grabbed at her heart at the most unexpected moments. She believed in God's will. She trusted His timing. And yet—she was human, too. Vanessa must love the children very much, so Courtney rejoiced with her. Why, then, did tears sting her eyes?

"Forgive me, Lord—oh, forgive me in the name of Your Son—for my sin is that of envy," she whispered, dropping into a chair in the sun room.

That is where Arabella Lovelace found her when the mail came. "You have a letter, dear—what is it, Courtney child? You look as if you have seen a ghost!"

I have, Cousin Bella—oh, I have! The ghost of my unborn child. The child who would be making May baskets today, Courtney's tortured heart cried out. But when she spoke, it was about her encounter with Horace Bellevue.

"He lacks my vote of confidence, too," Cousin Bella said through tight lips. "Perhaps I should speak with Clint. Give it no more thought, but be cautious. Now, enjoy your mail!"

The letter was from Lance—brief, to-the-point, and his writing looked cramped:

> My dear Courtney:
>
> Vanessa arrived just as I was leaving for your part of the world. And so it is that we will sojourn together. Your sister will be in need of an escort, believe me. The twins, Jordan and Jonda, are a handful to say the least. Gird your loins for battle.
>
> As always, my love,
>
> Lance

CHAPTER 10
"Somebody's Sister"

Spring gardens came into their own. Donolar's roses were at their peak. And still there was no word from Vanessa. Looking forward to the visit (it *was* only a visit, surely), Courtney felt both excited and apprehensive. Always glad to see Efraim and Roberta, she was doubly so when they appeared at church the last Sunday in May. It had been awhile since Efraim had attended. Business, he said. And, when her eyes met those of Horace Bellevue head-on, Courtney realized with a start that it had been longer still since he had been in attendance. Strange that his sudden appearance coincided with Efraim and Roberta's.

Oh, be fair, Courtney, she scolded inwardly, turning her glance away. *It is probably only a coincidence.*

But Clint's half brother pushed his way through the crowd as if driven and was effusive in his greeting. "Miss VanKoten! What an unexpected pleasure." He reached out and took her unproffered hands. "You do wonders for that suit. Right, Efraim?"

Courtney failed to hear her brother's reply. She was busy hurrying Roberta to where the Lovelaces, Mandy, and Mrs. Rueben were talking with Brother Jim.

"That was a soporific sermon this morning, Big Jimbo," Doc George grumbled. "Bottled, I could use it to induce sleep."

"George Washington!" Cousin Bella scolded. "It wasn't the sermon that put *you* into a doze. You were up half the night, listening to imaginary noises across the creek."

Doc George frowned slightly, but it was impossible for the unaccustomed crease between his bushy, white brows to linger. Shucking off the look of concern, he stroked his muttonchops in mock thoughtfulness. "The good woman has me imagining things now, good brother. You and Saint Paul were the wise ones—'Oh, when I was single, my pockets would jingle—' "

Brother Jim entered into the banter that the two life-long friends enjoyed. "Didn't want to be bearing down too hard today, observing as I did that the old soak, Lum Birdsey, darkened the door. Rumor has it he's bootleg-gin'—and I wouldn't put it past him. But I used a soft glove, hoping to get him into the ring before the Revs do!"

In some far recess of her mind Courtney heard a warning bell. What was troubling her? Something somebody had said—but what it was, if anything, eluded her.

"Ah must'a knowed y'all was a-comin' Mistah Efraim 'n Miz Roberta. Ah dun went'n made plum puddin' wid de fluffy, hard sauce dat's so sweet t'yore tongue."

Mandy rolled her eyeballs and licked her full lips in anticipation. Mrs. Rueben was not to be outdone. "*Der sauerkrat gut nahrung*—be you wid hunger—"

Efraim, who had joined them, took Roberta's arm. "How can we turn down such food?"

"We can't!" she said, giving him a tremulous smile.

Courtney turned back toward the church, her eyes searching for Clint. Somehow they had become sepa-rated. She spotted him talking with Horace Bellevue. Well, why not? The man was Clint's foreman. But Clint looked so serious, while his half brother's eyes, which always seemed to take in everything at once, wandered back to where Roberta stood with Efraim. Just in time, his gaze shifted to meet Clint's as they finished the conversation. For a moment, Clint appeared about to call Horace back. Then, his eyes catching Courtney's, he strode quickly to her side.

"Hello, beautiful!"

Courtney's heart gave an extra pump as inwardly she praised the Lord for him for what must be the millionth time.

Donolar, having ridden ahead on Pegasus, greeted the family at the door. "Look!" he said excitedly. "It's finished!"

And there in the foyer stood a high-back "settle" made of polished pine. On either side were heart-shaped, fabric-covered hearts. The beautiful bench was piled high with pillows, causing all to gasp in admiration. Donolar was pleased but puzzled.

"We're going to have company—somebody's sister, I think—"

CHAPTER 11
Fragment of a Nightmare

The grand meal coupled with the heady scent of Donolar's rose garden caused Clint's eyelids to droop. Courtney saw and suggested that he try to get a little rest.

"I admit being in a near-comatose state," Clint grinned. "Are you sure you don't mind, darling? I'm afraid I am poor company anyway." He hesitated in the foyer.

"Mind? I insist that you nap. It has been a grind at the mines. Just promise me a little corner in your dreams."

Poor darling. He looked exhausted. His face had lost the sun-bronze that spoke of the outdoors and his hands, when he reached out to touch her, were work-hardened. Small wonder, spending as much time as he did in the bowels of the earth.

Clint hugged her—hard. "M-m-m-m," he murmured into her hair, "M-m-m-m—"

"Clint!" she whispered, backing away, "we have an audience—"

Clint's full-bodied laugh removed ten years from his face. "I'm not tired anymore."

Pulse quickening at his touch, Courtney slipped from the comforting circle of his arms and backed away—right into a smiling Roberta. "Efraim is resting, too. We have been burning the midnight oil at the office—I sound just like a wife, don't I?" The girl's face colored fiercely.

"What is wrong with that?" Courtney smiled, throwing a fingertip kiss to Clint who was already halfway up the stairs.

Roberta looked confused. Trying to cover her embarrassment, she talked rapidly. "Dr. and Mrs. Lovelace are going calling—Mandy and Mrs. Rueben are going to a 'song fest' at one of the neighbor's—and—"

"I know their whereabouts. Roberta, what is wrong?"

"Nothing—nothing at all." Roberta was still breathless. "I—I thought this would be a good opportunity for me to check on Rambling Gate. The house has been unoccupied and the grounds neglected. Will you come with me?"

Each time someone made mention of the house with such a sordid past, Courtney felt a tingling in her veins. Why was it, she wondered, that more recent pleasantries faded so quickly from memory while nightmares, thought dead, resurfaced to cast their hypnotic spell? It was silly. Just plain silly.

"The air is glorious," she said. "The walk is just what the doctor ordered."

They were crossing the lawn and Roberta spun on the flagstone path to face her. "Oh Courtney, do you mean—are you—?"

"Pregnant? No," Courtney said sadly. "Would that I were. Sometimes I wonder if I am being punished—no, no, I know better than that—let us say I am being given a growing time in which to learn. You see, I still harbor the feeling of guilt, as if losing the baby were all my fault—"

"You know better! But I do understand about guilt and self-doubt—" Roberta paused and then asked if Courtney had talked over her feelings with Clint.

Well—yes and no. Why go over all that? Best concentrate on the glorious future.

Why burden her dear friend who had never known the joy of carrying another life within herself? How could she understand that Courtney who had everything (in Roberta's eyes) could find life narrow and colorless in comparison to those glorious days when she carried Clint's child?

Trees closed in around them and the sound of laughing waters foretold the knitting and purling of white foam dropped from the great heights of the mossy waterwheel at the top of its climb. The gloom thickened and Courtney felt the familiar chill creeping to her fingertips. Roberta must not have shared her haunting sense of another presence for, when she spoke, it was about a totally different matter. But equally disturbing.

"Courtney," Roberta said, pushing back a low-hanging hemlock bough and avoiding Courtney's eyes. "Wasn't that gallant of Horace Bellevue—you know, commenting on what I did for the suit, not what *it* did for *me*?"

Courtney stiffened. "He was right. Why should you think otherwise?"

"It's just that I—I still have not grown used to the new me. I can't thank you enough for the charm course!"

Roberta paused as the rail of the rustic bridge came into view. "Efraim sees me as an office fixture—and I guess I am in need of a compliment—do you understand?"

"Perfectly," Courtney answered, glancing furtively over her shoulder in an effort to allay her jitters. "But there are lots of men who would find you attractive—and that includes my brother. He is not one to flatter—like Horace Bellevue."

The all-seeing eyes of Rambling Gate were focused on the pair. "You don't like him, do you?" Roberta paused to ask.

"I don't trust him," Courtney said flatly.

There! The words were out. . . .

Roberta was right. Left alone, it was amazing how rapidly blackberry vines renewed their thorny fight for survival. Red with unripened fruit, they reached out as if to form a barrier between the two girls and the restored gambling hall. In the shadows, the great house appeared to have slunk back to its original state of decay—dark, dismal, and threatening—except for the towering acacia that flanked the front archway.

"Remember the ghost stories we used to hear about the big house, Roberta?" Courtney asked, feeling a need to break the silence.

Roberta laughed. "The bridge looks safe. I will go first—unless I hear footsteps rattle the planks!"

"Ghosts make no noise," Courtney said, trying to match her friend's bravado.

Roberta turned sideways to pick her way through an overgrown hedge along the walkway once they were safely across the bridge. "My, my! How weathered the place looks. The rainy winters have eaten away at the paint—let's have a look inside."

She fumbled in her bag, but there was no key to be found. "We used to keep an extra one under the flower pot by the windowbox—"

But there was no key. In fact, there was no pot.

Courtney felt an unexplainable sense of relief. She had no desire to enter the house. She felt a suffocating need to escape—else her taut nerves surely would snap like the strings of a violin. Looking up, she saw that spikes of crimson had been driven through the treetops by a lowering sun and Cousin Bella insisted on punctuality for the evening meal. They should leave now in order to make it by six o'clock—

But Roberta was not to be rushed. Noting that somebody had neglected to draw one of the drapes across the downstairs sitting room window, she motioned to Courtney. On leaden feet she joined Roberta and peered through the glass.

Furniture, shrouded in sheets, sat immobile, all as if to share their personal nightmares which made up the history of the Columbia Territory. The railroading Villards, when the inn was Gambling Gate, alive with drunken, coarse women, tankards of ale, and dice. The Bellevue Brothers and Alexis Worthington Villard Bellevue, holding the defenseless Mrs. Hillary (once a housekeeper for the Villards) as a front for their counterfeiting.

Well, the past was past. Why dwell on it? This country and its people had taught Courtney that valuable lesson. And yet . . . there was no escaping the future. What did the future hold for Rambling Gate?

Courtney wished Roberta would speak. The silence was eerie. But Roberta's face was a mask, as if there were something she wished to say but convention held her back.

Dear Roberta. She was so in love with Efraim that it made Courtney want to shake him. Forgetting her fear, she said softly, "You used to say this would be a beautiful place for a honeymoon. A little restoring and—"

"A *lot* of restoring," Roberta said with sadness in her voice. "I am glad that Dr. and Mrs. Lovelace had the place to themselves on their wedding night—but I guess I meant—well, I was thinking of memories to share with children—oh Courtney, I'm sorry, but there will be other children—for *you*—"

Courtney tried to laugh. "And soon! I guess Vanessa's twins are a handful—but—Roberta! Did you hear something?"

Roberta nodded wordlessly and pointed to the tanglewood behind the great house. "Something is going on—I—I feel it. I wish Father were here!" By unspoken agreement, they were hurrying across the bridge. And, in Courtney's mind, to safety.

CHAPTER 12
When Disaster Strikes

The two girls talked at length the next morning while Donolar helped Efraim hitch the horses to the carriage. Roberta was reluctant to return to the city. She disliked loose ends, she said, and Rambling Gate was just about the best example she could think of.

"Until I hear from my father, somebody should be there. And so much needs doing. Strange, but the place felt downright spooky even before we heard the noise."

Something clicked in Courtney's memory. "The noise could have been some prowling animal, Roberta—at least, I would have told myself so had it not been for Doc George's report of sounds coming from across the stream. Talk it over with Efraim," she suggested.

It was Efraim who told her three days later of Roberta's decision. Efraim had brought papers needing Clint's signature verifying that miners in his employ were to share in the profits and dropped by to see his sister. "Dropped by" hardly covered it. Efraim had made a special trip. And small wonder. His face showed little emotion; but there was an underlying current of anger in his voice.

"Horace Bellevue will be in charge of Rambling Gate—"

"Horace Bellevue! Efraim, are you out of your mind!"

"It is not up to me to make Miss VanKoten's choices." His voice was low but sharp.

"*Miss VanKoten!*" Courtney felt her eyes widen with

shock as she stared at this pale-faced stranger before her. "What has happened between you two?"

"Nothing has happened! I have tried to tell you that before—" Efraim fingered the lapel of his double-breasted, khaki jacket uncertainly a moment. Then he was Efraim Glamora, attorney-at-law again. Matter closed.

"How will he manage—both jobs, I mean?" She was still trying to understand.

"That, little sister," he said gently, "is up to the young lady, your husband, and Horace Bellevue—"

Neither of them had seen Donolar enter the Mansion's front garden where they were standing. His startling scream was one of terror. "The Brothers! My butter-flies—oh, something awful will happen now—some disaster—"

It took both of them to calm their brother.

But Courtney was far from calm. Some disaster? It had struck already.

CHAPTER 13
The End of the World?

For Courtney, it had been a sleepless night. The third in succession that Clint was unable to leave the mines. So much depended on the success of the new veins. But she was lonely. And a little afraid. The mystery at Rambling Gate unnerved her. But something else niggled—oh yes, the recurring dream. It was the same, always the same. She had given birth to a near-perfect baby, but both she and her newborn were submerged in roiling waters. Courtney tried desperately to hold the baby's head above the surface but felt herself sinking lower . . . lower . . . lower . . . until the beautiful child was swept from her arms. And Clint was not there.

Wiping the cold beads of perspiration from her brow with the sleeve of her nightgown, Courtney welcomed the rising sun, watched it pick out the trees near the bedroom window, first giving them shape and then color. She realized then that the lamp was still burning, its light pallid in contrast to the morning sun. She had fallen asleep reading the Bible, her finger still marking one of her and Clint's favorite bedtime passages:

> For I am persuaded, that neither death nor life, nor angels, nor principalities, nor powers, nor things present, nor things to come, nor height, nor depth, nor any other creature, shall be able to separate us from the love of God, which is in Christ Jesus our Lord.

Romans 8 . . . how it brightened their Christian hope.

"Thank You, Lord, for the reassurance. And Lord, I thank You with all my heart that the awful nightmare is fading. Now, put the words in my mouth as I try to bring this same hope to the Thorsons whose cabin was destroyed by fire. In the name of Jesus. Amen."

Brother Jim was waiting beneath a vault of blinding blue sky. What a morning! How could anyone guess that the fig tree would regret that she had put forth her green leaves?

They had gone but a little way when Brother Jim pointed ahead and said in surprise, "Why, if it isn't Lum—rubbery-legged and in need of a scouring. Guess we'd best give him a lift before he falls on his face. On the wagon, my foot!"

Lum Birdsey, eyes red-laced and rimmed from lack of sleep, staggered aboard, mumbling an apology for the way he "smelt." Been all night lookin' fer Horace Bellevue who wuz a-gonna give 'im some work—kinda lost his directions. . . .

"Course you did, my good man! Throw that jug of stinking hooch in the thicket and start sobering up. Otherwise, you are bound for one monumental hangover, man! You promised me you'd be giving religion a try—"

The weasely little man hung his head. What a sorry sight. The long gray hair was tousled and matted beneath a ragged, shapeless felt hat. The grizzled gray-and-white chin undoubtedly itched the way his greasy hands kept clawing at it. His clothes were wretchedly dirty. And his breath was foul with the stale odor of alcohol.

"I guess likker's me religion, parson," he said pitifully. "I guess deprivin' me ud cause me t'put a bullet right 'twixt my eyes."

At Brother Jim's command, the horse lurched forward. "Nobody told you it would be easy, Lum. The narrow path never is. You're right. You're hooked, good and proper. No way you can stop guzzlin' the poison by yourself. But with God as your partner, now that's different. Right, Courtney?"

Courtney gulped, hoping that her feelings did not show. She was sick from the odor of their passenger. And her mind was still stuck on his mission. What had Horace Bellevue promised this piece of humanity whom only God could help?

"You are worthy in God's sight," she mumbled, feeling a little hypocritical.

Lum Birdsey took heart. "Guess I be 'bout as good as some what go whoopin' 'n yellin' them *amens*."

"Don't go excusin' yourself, Lum. The Lord's not bent on makin' comparisons in His judgment. Where was it you wanted to go?"

The man appeared to hesitate. When he answered, the name was almost a whisper. "Mr. Bellevue—I need t'see 'im."

"Oh, Horace Bellevue—he's apt to be at the mines—"

"Or possibly at Rambling Gate," Courtney supplied, half regretting that she knew.

At her words, Lum Birdsey visibly shrank. It was as if he were struck dumb. Did Brother Jim feel it, too? There was a trenchant pause as the horse stumbled and the buggy swayed as it swung back and forth between ruts lacing the country road together. . . .

Courtney, deep in thought, forgot to wonder where or why the big preacher was taking Lum Birdsey. The tent, temporary quarters for John and Della Thorrson since the fire, was just over the rise when, without warning, there was an earthshaking jolt. Thunder? From a clear sky?

Only the sapphire sky was no longer visible! Black clouds, fat with rain, had bunched together to obliterate the sun. And then, with unbelievable speed, a blue-green cloud appeared from nowhere, massing the smaller clouds, robbing them of all individuality, and centering right overhead like a black veil of mourning. Lightning rent the black veil, followed so immediately by an explosion of thunder that the three in the ancient buggy knew the strike was close even before the tallest of the fir trees just ahead split in half and crashed to the ground.

"Get out of the buggy and run for the tent!" Brother Jim's booming voice was barely audible above the shriek of the wind which pushed them back when they would have climbed out. Dust devils formed, sucking at their clothes.

And then the wind stopped. The dust settled. And the pines stopped sighing, each needle frozen in position. Waiting. Again the lightning, leaving a heated wave of compression along the trail of its strike. The horse whinnied and reared crazily in spite of Brother Jim's hands on the reins.

"Run for it!" he commanded, trying to restrain the steed. But Lum was beyond moving. "He's after me—th' Lord God Almighty's aimin' at me, like Jonah. Throw me t'th' giant fish—"

Courtney, too, felt frozen—knowing that they were in the path of the storm and unable to escape it the way one is unable to command the body in a nightmare. She could only will her hand to point at the black curtain draping from the sky to meet the horizon all around them. Rain. There would be buckets. There would be barrels. She had heard of situations in which it rained fish. Maybe, she thought crazily, they should hope for one big enough to swallow Lum Birdsey—if the clouds were indeed in league against him.

"Go!" Brother Jim was screaming. But it was too late. And, as it happened, it would have done no good to flee. . . .

In less time than it took to tell Clint when the menacing storm was over, the black curtain turned white.

White with hail. Ice stones as big as the apples which, full-grown, were beginning to ripen. Like leaden balls from a deadly cannon, they struck Courtney's head, bare since the wind had stolen her silken scarf. They struck the horse causing the animal to rear, wild-eyed in fear. Fending off the icy attack as best as he could with one elbow over his head and the other wrapped around the neck of the frantic horse, Brother Jim unhitched the animal and tugged him to the nearest tree. There he tethered him, having decided that the hail stones posed more certain danger than a possible lightning strike.

Brother Jim gestured and Courtney understood his signal for her to crawl beneath the flimsy buggy. The storm went on forever, beating at the improvised roof the buggy bed made like a thunderous drum. Closing out the rest of the sounds of the snorting, whinnying horse who watched the scene from a wall-eyed stance as the ice bruised and battered his flesh until it was raw and bleeding.

"Is it the end of the world?" Lum Birdsey whimpered, his eyes as wild as the horse's.

"Could be—very well could be!" Brother Jim had to shout to be heard. "It will come like a thief in the night. And I daresay that it's the end of the world for some all right—"

Even as he spoke, there was a mighty blast of wind with screams of horror riding its arctic wings. And then something resembling the Magic Carpet of Arabian Night tales whizzed by. The Thorson tent!

CHAPTER 14
Aftermath

The clouds shrank and departed, pausing only long enough to paint a gloriously beautiful rainbow glowing from horizon to horizon and reflecting almost mockingly on a sea of glass. How deceptively innocent it all looked. Until one dared cast an eye on the road paved with hailstones. The foot-deep mounds of them heaped in the sagging buggy. And the barren knoll where the Thorson tent used to be.

Brother Jim opened the lid on back of his buggy with a bang and pulled out a musty-smelling blanket. "Wrap this around your being while I try unsnarling the reins I twisted around the brake. Give me a hand with Lum here." Lum Birdsey's sausage-like fingers clung to the axle of the buggy and he kept his jump-jack squatting position even after they had positioned him on the ground. "Lightning might as well have struck him—he's scared out of his senses—bless his alcoholic soul!"

The big preacher barked out orders. Satan must have unleashed all the demons of Hades. But good, like the sun, always won out and—by jiminy—the three of them were placed here just in time to give the good Lord a hand. And they jolly well better abide lest the second condition be worse than the first!

The suggestion brought Lum to his senses. He took a tobacco pouch from his pocket, bit off an enormous chunk of the brown contents, then—looking at the sky— spat it out.

"The Thorsons—what about them?" Courtney dared to ask at last. "There's a baby—" She shuddered, remembering her haunting dream.

"We have to find them. The horse here's spooked—not safe for a woman to drive. I'll try and find help. If the two of you can start looking—let me be warning you that what you find may not be a pretty sight—"

"We'll manage," Courtney said, wondering if they could. A woman frightened out of her wits and a drunken man.

"Somebody may come along, but don't go bankin' on it. You're mostly on your own—looking for that poor woman—just be trusting yourself, Courtney. A woman needs a woman in such times. And you, Lum," Brother Jim's big fist doubled up for a right-hand punch, "that booze may come in right handy, after all—*for Mrs. Thorson!* She's apt to be in shock. Administer about a teaspoonful—and *you*, if you touch one drop, I'll be sniffing it. And may those demons make a special trip back just for you!"

Courtney had never felt so lonely in her entire life as when Brother Jim's buggy drove away—the horse snorting and the wobbling wheels crunching loudly on the hailstones. "Dear God, be with us all," she whispered.

The ice melted quickly, but the ground was slippery and the lowering sun made it difficult to see. The sound of wagon wheels cheered Courtney as she and Lum searched and called to no avail. At Courtney's frantic waving, the driver pulled alongside the road and looked at the two of them quizzically. The occupants were strangers and Courtney took no time for an exchange of pleasantries.

"Help us—oh, please help us! There has been a terrible tragedy here—"

"Lady, they's been uh trag'dy ever'whares—me'n my

family's cleaned out an'll be lookin' fer greener pastures. Th' storm was general—all over this forsaken state, I guess—all th' wheat's gone—"

The wheat. The wheat was *gone*?

"Plum destroyed—th' wheat . . . gardens . . . even kilt th' chickens . . . new calves . . . and some mares 'bout to foal. . . ."

The vision floated before Courtney's eyes. There would be no golden harvest. Even the dread smut would be preferred to this. The way she understood it, the spores hid in the heads of the grain until, like sin in mankind's weakest moment, they took over—slimy with decay— destroying the entire crop. A rain could trigger the disease. Or winds could transport the spores. But surely there was some way to keep the entire crop, as well as the neighbors', from taint, Courtney had insisted when Clint told her this was the farmers' worst enemy. Yes, they could burn it—controlled burning by means of fireguards. Of course, the sour stench was worse than Lum's still (if bootlegging he was). Yes, the whole valley could become contaminated. And there were insects to battle, but arsenic helped control them.

All this Courtney had understood. But the *weather.* Nobody could control that.

The vision of golden harvests with all the men singing "Bringing in the Sheaves" faded. The green glory of promise was gone—every blade driven into the earth from which it came. . . .

And Mandy's garden! What of her cucumbers, the bush limas, and the string beans that had reached the top of the stakes . . . the honeydews that were in full bloom? And what about the orchards? Gone was the fruit. And the trees, stripped of their limbs, might succumb as well.

Surely, this must be the worst thing that could happen. How wrong she was!

They found the baby first. Its little body blue with cold, the lifeless bit of humanity lay beside a mossy log—its unseeing eyes tilting upwards as if in search of the mother. Courtney picked the baby up, wrapped the fragile body in the rough blanket Brother Jim had left, and stumbled forward—forward to where Della Thorson lay just inches away.

There was a breath of life remaining. Courtney was almost sure she saw a single rise and fall of the bony rib cage. But the neck went off to one side crazily beneath the splintered limb of the tree that lightning had struck.

"Della, Della," Courtney whispered. "Don't give up—"

The eyes were blank. Dead. The rest of her could not be far behind. Holding back tears that threatened to drown her, Courtney laid the baby against its mother's breast. With one last feeble effort, Della Thorson inhaled shallowly, holding the breath in her lungs. Gently, the unseeing eyes closed, like the petals of a cornflower whose day is done. But there was the hint of a smile on the pallid face. She and her baby were reunited. . . .

There was the sound of horses' hooves. Close. But to Courtney a million miles away. She was still kneeling beside mother and child, her eyes dry with unshed tears, when the boom of Brother Jim's voice shattered the deadly still.

Lum Birdsey had lifted the bottle to his dry lips, dealing with death in the only way he knew how. Draining it, he slunk into the underbrush to be seen no more. But Brother Jim's voice followed him down into the canyon.

"Poison, poison!" the giant preacher was screaming. He, too, was trying to cope. To understand before he was able to help others. "Get out of those trees, the rest of you Thorson children. Come!"

And then tender arms enfolded Courtney. Clint! She let him hold her as she wept for the loss of life. The wheat was symbolic. It had perished . . . as had this family . . . as had the life she had once sheltered. *All before their time. . . .*

CHAPTER 15
An Hour of Darkness

Della Thorson was laid to rest on the little knoll where the tent had stood. The bereaved widower stood a little apart from the large group that gathered to help, his arms around the surviving children, his face twitching in pain.

Brother Jim, with less than his usual ceremony, commended mother and child "back into the loving arms of God from whence they came." His trembling voice gathered strength as he reassured Josh Thorson that his family would be cared for—as would all others in need in this hour of darkness. Already, Arabella Lovelace was opening her house to those whose cabin roofs had blown off. And Clint Desmond, God's handyman, was making room at the mines for extra men. The Lord would provide for the faithful. If the men would like to meet with him at the church to do some praying and planning . . .

Widder Roundtree took the orphaned Thorsons home with her and the men followed Brother Jim in the direction of the Church-in-the-Wildwood. Clint stayed behind momentarily.

"I must go, too, sweetheart. There's so much to do—"

"I know," Courtney whispered against his chest. "I know."

"There are no words to tell you how proud of you I am—and," his voice broke, "no words to tell God how thankful I am that you were not harmed—"

"I know—I know," she said again, burying her tearful face against the security of his suit coat. "I—I did what I had to do—all the while thinking of the brevity of life, how precious every moment is. I can never take life for granted again—never. The experience will be with me always—oh Clint, hold me, hold me *tight!*"

Clint's strong arms closed around her and for one precious moment she listened to the heavy thudding of his heart. Then, with an effort, she gently pushed him away. God had embued him with the foresight which could save the entire valley. He had no choice but to put it to use. Clint—dear, wonderful Clint—the husband who had taught her that while salvation could happen in a twinkling, discipleship took a lifetime of learning and practicing . . . even in the darkest hour.

Head held high, Courtney turned toward the Mansion. She, too, was called to God's service. No, life would never be the same. Henceforth, she would place herself completely at the Master's disposal. The world around her was in shambles, but the dove of peace had found a resting place in her heart.

CHAPTER 16
Manna—and Quails

It was dark when Courtney entered the Mansion. Even the wicks of the lamps were turned low in respect to the dead. But there was frenzied activity inside. Donolar had boarded up windows in which the glass was broken by the hail. He had patched the roof where shakes were blown off and sawed a lightning-struck tree into firewood for Mandy's kitchen range. The monster was always hungry, holding its mouth open like a giant fledgling waiting to be fed.

And now the house was bulging with refugees whose losses had been far greater than the Mansion suffered. The east wing was open, as was the tower. How good that the great historic home—with all its peculiar wings, curves, and added-on ells—could accommodate so many. For how long—who knew?

"We'll live it a day at a time," Cousin Bella said. Dear, hospitable Cousin Bella, who would be as much alone for however long it took her doctor-husband to mend bones as Courtney would be while Clint worked with renewed strength at the mines.

"Where do butterflies go when it rains?" Courtney asked Donolar on what must have been their thousandth trip up the stairs to carry quilts and blankets.

"Oh, they are smart—my butterflies. They fly over the bridge between Innisfree and Eden. They were never cast out. There's a special butterfly bush there to protect them."

"What a beautiful thought," Courtney murmured, wondering if Donolar's sister would be more receptive to his creative mind and pure-of-heart thinking than their mother had been. Vanessa! Oh, somebody must try and stop her before she came during this time of crisis.

There was no further time for thinking. The men were coming back from the church, some of their voices booming with hope which only a few hours ago had seemed dead.

Mandy bustled out of the kitchen. Her perspiring black face was as shiny as a wet seal. In contrast, her forearms were white with flour to the elbows. "Din-nah's 'bout t'be ready. I dun baked some, 'cause time's a-comin' when dey's gonna be no flour—"

"Ve fin' der flour—even if der brice be bretty taller'n vun hund dog. Ve ride to der fort, 'bout vivteen miles. Ve ride to der city, but ve vind vot ve von't, *nicht*?"

It was one of the few times Mrs. Rueben had been known to speak out publicly, although—when dealing with the cook—the German housekeeper's tongue was honed to rival the sharpness and surety of an archer's arrow.

Even now, although she spoke to anyone in need of reassurance, Mrs. Rueben cast a withering glance at Mandy. Let the valley sit up and take notice that these people would not starve—long as they remembered to clean off their boots ere tracking her freshly scrubbed floors.

"Humph!" Mandy snorted, which translated into *Who does she think she is?* Then, with a wide, pearly-toothed grin, she scored another point. "Coffee's dun ready—fresh-ground—'n fresh-biled by mah own han's!"

The hot brew loosened men's tongues. As the talk droned around her, Courtney found herself increasingly surprised at the humble appreciation of some of the men and the ingratitude of others. Certainly, the recent events were tragic. But were they unable to see that matters could have been worse—so much worse?

"Ever'thang's gone—tooken without notice . . . The weather don' hafta give no notice . . . Th' Lord wuz good—savin' my family fer me . . . Th' Lord'd be good no matter iffen He took 'em . . . *But what'er we a-gonna do*?"

Clint set his cup down quietly. His face was chalky, but his voice was steady. "I thought we charted our plans at the church, men. We can survive another year if we stand together, but we'll have to remember as we said back there that we *are* our brother's keeper! We will share by pooling our resources. Most likely we can provide temporary work for most of you men at the mines—"

"I'm a farmer—not a gopher diggin' holes," one man interrupted. "I'll be gatherin' my wife 'n kids then with our belongin's we gonna head back whur we shudda stayed!"

Clint's lips tightened and his eyes were unnaturally bright. "Nobody is a captive here. You are all free to go. But we urge you to stay. The ground is rich with minerals and the soil is fertile. We can build back. Those of you with loans outstanding can pay with wages then float new loans for next year's planting—"

"Wages—ain't ye bitin' off more'n ye can chaw?"

"Maybe—maybe I am. But the Lord willing, we will make it. We owe it to our families to try. If we cling to our faith, maybe we can turn the catastrophe into a triumph. We voted, but let's have an 'aye' again for those willing to try."

Courtney had never been so proud of her husband as when the *ayes* rocked the rafters. Some were not to be put down, of course. And for the dissenters, Brother Jim had a few well-chosen words.

"Why, you ingrates! You mumbling-grumbling wanderers of the wilderness! Me and the Lord should take you on for a bare-fisted 14-rounder. Now, the situation's less than perfect, but why harp on what we all know? I'm ashamed of your sour, petty attitudes—*wimpy's* a mild word for you. Now, apologize before Clint here changes his mind!" A murmur of apology, then Brother Jim spoke again. "Now, it's time we partake of Mandy's manna. And (triumphantly) it's no accident there's quail! God sent us a whole covey like for the children of Israel. *Is it well with thee?*"

CHAPTER 17
The Long Road Back

It would be a long, slow road back.

The storm had been far more devastating than at first supposed. Everything lay in ruins around her as Courtney ran the short distance between the Mansion and the Laughten cabin. Rail fences were down, giving the few surviving cattle open range. Now, lowing pitifully for their lost young, they grazed halfheartedly at the few cornstalks which, stripped of their blades, bent earthward like grieving skeletons. Loss of the corn had hurt Mandy worst of all. It was ready to "ear" and what she would give for "roas' 'nears" before stalks were cut for fodder or declared forbidden fruit—reserved for the stock's winter feed, next year's seed, and pots of hominy to serve with pork chops after the potatoes in the root cellar gave out. Courtney wondered just how much corn was in reserve. Cornmeal was an important staple once the wheat was gone. What, she wondered, would happen to the gristmill? Abner Tompkins made his living just taking a handful of flour as payment for grinding wheat into flour. Ahab would grind the corn—if any remained —for cornmeal.

Gardens, like the wheat, were beaten into the earth. Already the musty smell of rotting cabbage and carnage lay heavy on the once rare, clean breeze. Some of the cabins, stripped of their siding, stood like empty rib cages. Others were destroyed completely. And everywhere the ground was littered with shredded bedding and clothing.

Maybe the man who had spoken out was right. Maybe Clint *had* taken on too much. Then she brushed the thought away and squared her shoulders. God had never needed her so much. For it was she who must keep Clint encouraged when hope seemed gone.

Buried in thought, Courtney failed to hear Cara's first call of welcome. "Miz—I mean Courtney—how good o' you t'come! We wuz luckier'n most—not much damage and I'm ready t'show th' Lord my 'preciation. Some folks ain't got no clothes—"

"Bless you, Cara," Courtney said. "That is partly why I called. If you would be willing to bring your sewing machine, Cousin Bella has bought a lot of material— enough that, added to the outgrown children's clothes some have brought, I believe we can at least get the women and children dressed."

"I understand some come runnin' t'shelter wrapped in bed sheets—"

The practical Cara was already assembling thread and needles. If Courtney could carry the baby, she could manage the other two children—and could Donolar help move the machine?

Courtney nodded and the two, laden with far more than frail arms should carry, hurried to where Donolar was sowing turnips and setting out collards slips for a fall garden.

" 'It is not enough to help the feeble up, but to support him after,' " Donolar said. "I wonder if Shakespeare meant to plant a garden—oh yes, the sewing machine— and I must tell my butterflies that the hail shredded the rhododendrons in the glen but not their roses—"

He stopped suddenly. "Did you see the new snow?"

Courtney gasped when she looked upward at the surrounding mountains. Imagine such a blanket at this time of year.

"And did you see *him*—the Brother?" The wide, expressionless eyes enlarged until they were mirrors reflecting the waste around them.

Horace! For the first time, Courtney wondered where Clint's half brother was when all the planning was in progress. Surely, her eyes had simply failed to see him in the hordes of half-crazed people. As Clint's foreman, Horace Bellevue had to be among them—lending Clint a hand—

But, to Courtney's surprise, Cara said innocently, "Mr. Bellevue's been a-helpin' at Ramblin' Gate—him and that pore Mr. Lum what takes t'th' bottle so much. They work a lots at night, I think."

Courtney wondered later just how much more Cara knew. Her talk was cut short by Courtney's gasp as she stumbled over the bloated carcass of a cow—and then another. Oh, surely she was not going to be sick. Swallowing hard, she tried not to hear Cara say, "They plan on burnin' th' dead animals tomorrow—'cause of disease, y'know—"

CHAPTER 18
Changes

❦

The beautiful tradition of the Mansion was shattered. No more leisurely candlelight dinners. Even the grandfather clock and its echo, the cuckoo clock, were silent since time had lost its meaning. Cousin Bella's sun room was turned into a bedroom temporarily (although nobody seemed able to define the meaning of the word). In fact, the mistress of Mansion-in-the-Wild was seldom home. Disregarding her own physical limitations, Arabella Lovelace now accompanied the doctor on his endless rounds. There had been countless injuries, followed by the usual epidemic of spring maladies of whooping cough, measles, and chicken pox, and then the worst of all—some kind of unidentified sickness that Doc Lovelace could only attribute to pollution. Could be typhoid, he admitted glumly, and hung quarantine signs on the doors of cabins in which members of the family were victims. There no longer were public meetings for fear of spreading the dread disease.

Throwing caution to the wind, Cousin Bella kept her husband's pace, taking along food and a change of bedding. The Lovelaces often met with Brother Jim who did for the soul what Doc George did for the flesh. In one of these encounters, the three of them decided it wise to bury those who succumbed quietly and without an audience. Hopefully, this would help control the spread. Hopefully, too, it would avoid panic. Things were bad enough already.

Courtney divided her time between helping Mandy to cook, Mrs. Rueben to clean, and Cara to sew. Then, there was cleaning of the debris on the grounds surrounding the Mansion. And, certainly, Donolar was wise in thinking ahead to a fall garden. She spent hours squatting to help him break clods and plant seeds he thought would germinate before the first freeze. Her hands grew rough and reddened and every muscle in her small body ached. And, inside, her heart ached for Clint . . . Clint and their plans . . . their dreams.

There were nights when, from sheer exhaustion, she crept upstairs to escape the around-the-clock whirring of the sewing machine, the smell of food, and the endless talk of wives whose losses were far greater than her own, just to stand before her mirror momentarily. At such times, she would sigh sadly and hopelessly at the black aura of hair encircling her head—so disheveled and unappealing. Almost fiercely then she would grab her hairbrush and stroke her hair until it flowed, glistening and black as a starless night, from the center part Clint loved. If only—if only—he could walk in unexpectedly. . . .

But that never happened. Clint was assigning men to jobs at the mine. Clint was ordering supplies for families whose homes were uninhabitable. Clint was talking to Efraim, asking that he check the status of the loans which farmers had hoped to repay with the harvest which would never materialize.

"Things are going well," Efraim told Courtney in one of their few moments together. "That husband of yours is a wonder-worker when it comes to organizing—but the both of you look exhausted. Rest, my darling—"

But courage and determination were like a rock inside her. So Courtney waved aside her brother's pleas.

"You're more than all right in my book," Efraim said, shaking his head at the small face so full of newborn strength, so shining, so steadfast in spite of the loneliness and fatigue she must be feeling.

He must be going he said. But Courtney detained him with a question. "Efraim, what about Horace Bellevue? Is he what he says he is—I mean, is he working for Clint—and is he dependable?"

Efraim's jaw tightened. "I don't know what his arrangement is with Clint. The man has made several trips to my office inquiring about the loans—offering to float some of them, I understand, not to me but to the creditors—"

"But where would he get that kind of money?"

"Ask Miss VanKoten!"

He spun on his heel and was gone. Those were the first curt words Efraim Glamora had ever spoken to the sister he adored.

Three days passed. And then three weeks. One by one families were moving back into their cabins. But a month had passed and Courtney had not seen her husband.

When Doc George, busier than ever, asked Courtney if she would have Donolar take her to the fort for medical supplies, she quickly consented. But, back of her mind, a plan had formed. She would say nothing of the trip to her brother. There was no danger in her riding alone. And she would ride like the wind, she thought as she saddled Peaches, in order to detour and see Clint on the way home.

At the fort, Courtney found a lot of changes. All damages were repaired. Two new regiments had moved in (most of the soldiers ogling her with unnerving grins). A dentist had hung out a sign: TEETH PULLED HERE, ONE BUCK APIECE, TWO FOR $1.50 SPECIAL TODAY! There were other buildings, too, one with a whiskey barrel for a chimney. But the drugstore—where was it? A grinning boy pointed down the creaky boardwalk and said something about its being past the poker hall. But Courtney paid little attention in her hurry to finish here.

That was a mistake. Five minutes later, she had pushed open a pair of bat-wing doors and entered a darkened room. Dozens of men, hats pulled low over their eyes, sat around a poker table. The fermented air was filled with smoke and foul language. Then there was sudden silence, followed by a series of insulting whistles.

A swarthy man, wearing a grease-streaked apron around his bulging belly and a mustache that made him pass for a walrus, sauntered up to Courtney.

"You comin' in t'sing hymns, lady?"

Crude laughter.

Courtney drew herself up to her full height. "I am looking for the drugstore. If you will direct me, please—"

He grinned to show rotting teeth. "Want I should walk you the two blocks east—"

Turning her face away to avoid the stale, liquor-laden breath, Courtney pulled the pleats of her riding skirt around her knees to avoid contact with the squinting men who were now boldly extending their hands to delay her.

She ran the two blocks and entered the drugstore breathlessly. To her surprise, she saw above the rows of bottles and boxes a sign reading: RING BELL FOR SERVICE—THE DOCTOR WILL BE RIGHT OUT. Doctor—not druggist?

A tap of the bell brought a man whose sparse frame made him appear seven feet tall. His gray-green eyes viewed the world from behind round-lensed, nose-pinching spectacles—at the moment focused upon her quizzically. The cloth jacket he wore was as white as the shock of unruly hair that fell forward, bouncing to keep time with his every word.

"Howdy, ma'm. I'm Doctor Ramsey. You must be new—bearing no resemblance to the poor sod-buster wives."

The voice placed him south of the Mason-Dixon line—warm, sympathetic, thick as sludge. To emphasize his point, Doctor Ramsey inclined his head toward a scrubbed window by which passed a line of dispirited, forlorn women. "Sad souls. A doctor can tell a lot about a woman by how she carries herself. Follow me. My office is in back."

His office? The man had mistaken her for a patient. But Courtney found herself following. Obviously intelligent and well-informed, maybe he could answer the questions Doc George was unable or unwilling to. Babies were smarter than mothers, he kept insisting. They had their own sense of timing and joined the human race when they grew curious about all the adult hoopla. And maybe the good Lord needed a new pattern.

Feeling a little disloyal to Doc George, Courtney hesitated once she was inside the clean, antiseptic-scented office. Oh well, a second opinion was always wise.

"What are your symptoms?" Doctor Ramsey asked once she had given her name and let him help her onto the examining table. Symptoms? She had none. She was in good health. So—

"Why am I unable to conceive?" Courtney asked shyly.

Efficiently, almost indifferently, the doctor thumped here and there and made use of his countless instruments. But he seemed reluctant to make a diagnosis.

"Lots of scar tissue," he said almost to himself. "Have you aborted?"

"*Aborted!*" Courtney was startled, then angry. "Why, my husband and I want a child more than anything else in the world. I—I came here for help—and—"

Courtney was unable to go on, but the doctor was unabashed. Could he have brought so many babies into the world that it was routine—if not downright boring? But, given his background and experience, the man should know that to the prospective parents, their baby is—if not the world's first—the world's most important!

Doctor Ramsey removed his glasses and pressed a dimple into his unbearded chin with a thoughtful forefinger. "It's healthy seeing a young woman welcome motherhood. But it's difficult when a doctor must be discouraging. First, let me explain that nature aborts that which might not make it in the outside world. I never intended implying that you were responsible. However, I'm neither sure that you could or should become pregnant again—"

"You mean—" Courtney gave a little cry and sprang from the table.

"I mean—there are things a doctor can do—no? Then, my courageous young lady, leave it to Mother Nature."

"I will leave it to God!"

Maybe he was competent. Maybe not. Courtney thanked him when he refused a fee, saying he had done nothing. He then filled her order, looking at her curiously. Here was a strange case . . . but who was he to ask questions? Blinded by tears, the beautiful lady rushed out. This would be a good time for her to talk to her husband.

But Courtney thought otherwise.

CHAPTER 19
"Great Day in De Mawnin'!"

Another week passed before Clint was able to leave the Kennedy Mines in the charge of Brother Jim and Horace Bellevue and get home to Courtney. During those seven days Courtney kept up an ongoing conversation with God. There was no time to steal away to some dark closet, so she prayed on the run. Added to the seemingly endless work of restoration, there were two other events which dug into her time. First—to nobody's surprise, Cousin Bella told her—Josh Thorson married the Widder Roundtree. A good arrangement, everybody said. The poor man had need of a mother for all those little ones. And the widow—well, it was no secret that she was well-off, in need of nothing, except a husband.

While it would not be "proper-like" to have a real shivaree, there should be food taken to the cabin. And, goodness knows, those poor children had never had a toy in their lives. Now some whittled-out blocks and a rag doll or so . . .

Courtney helped with it all, envying the new Mrs. Thorson a little when she saw the round little faces light up with joy over the toys. As Mrs. Roundtree, the new bride had been denied children, too. So her face was as alive with happiness as were the children's.

Then Roberta came. There was little chance for talking. She must get to Rambling Gate and check on progress there, she said a little evasively. But she helped Courtney with some errands which gave them a few minutes.

"Efraim is livid about Horace Bellevue's being around," she confided. "But he does not understand, Courtney—"

"Neither do I."

"It isn't like you think—there's nothing going on—"

"When Horace Bellevue's around there is always something going on!"

They had parted with too much left unspoken. Or maybe too much *had* been spoken. They were both so tired.

Courtney, still praying her endless prayer in the secret chambers of her heart, paused long enough to change the subject. "Forgive me, Lord. I love Roberta—it's just that I fear what could happen. Take care of her until I can tell her I am sorry."

And then she resumed her entreaty for a child. Later . . . much, much later . . . she was to look back on this time as being proof perfect of the power of prayer. And to marvel at the mystery in which the Creator replies. . . .

* * *

Most of the valley folk having gone their separate ways, the Mansion was quiet. Only one family remained, and volunteers would have the logs of their cabin chinked by mid-afternoon. Clint had sent word by one of the helpers that he would be home for the night.

One would think the President was coming, Courtney smiled to herself, judging by the flurry of activity once the last guests waved good-bye. Mrs. Rueben was changing sheets in frenzied haste and had set the giant black washpot to boiling even though it was Friday instead of Monday. Mandy concentrated on the bill o' fare for the evening meal.

"Mistah Clint he be takin' uh likin' t'mah leek soup and ah'm a-gonna add poached salmon wid creamed taters, hush puppies, wilted-down lettuce what hid 'neath de 'zalia bush—'n den finish dinnah off wid mah apple-'n-bramble pie—'n whur'n tarnation did dem barrel-size coffee mugs go hidin'?"

Alone at last in the upstairs suite so long denied Courtney and Clint, she pressed her face lovingly against the cool comfort of the woodwork, remembering the intimate moments and the hours of dreaming they had shared in these quarters. With one foot she moved a bright rag rug to Clint's side of the bed. He loved to put his feet on its cozy softness at the start of day. And, of course, the two easy chairs overlooking the garden should be moved closer together.

But the rest of the time, what little remained, she must spend on herself. Minutes later, Courtney liked what the ancient oval mirror reflected. Freshly scrubbed, her face was clear and glowing, the firm mouth pleasantly pink, and her dark eyes—once sad—were still too large for her face, but their dark depths were bright with anticipation. Her hands—well, there was little she could do about them. Work had taken its toll. But her hair, hanging to her shoulders the way Clint liked it best, still shone above the pink ruffle of a cool voile blouse.

Time had not changed her, the mirror said—except for the better. Inside, she was different and the difference reflected in her eyes. What, she wondered, was that subtle difference?

And then she knew! God had delivered her from the grip of inferiority, self-doubt, and guilt. Strange how it had taken her this long to recognize the change. The old Courtney would have crawled back into the shell of despair when Doctor Ramsey spoke of abortion and the danger of another pregnancy. The new Courtney looked back with no remorse and forward with no fear. There would be a buttercup baby who was disgustingly healthy . . . the apple of his father's eye. . . .

Courtney's dream was cut short by a rap on the door.

Recognizing the *rat-a-tat-tat* signal, she called out breathlessly, "*Clint!* Oh, my darling, when are you going to stop that silly knocking? We are married—remember?"

Clint rushed in.

"*Remember!*" His warm breath widened the part of her hair and for a moment of unutterable sweetness they melted into each other's arms. Only to have the clock strike six!

There was something different about dinner, something that sent a quiver along Courtney's nerves, cut short her breath. Although she could never have explained why as Mandy, in Brother Jim's absence, read the Scriptures in her rich dialect, it was as if the time of waiting were drawing to a close. Throughout the delectable dinner, the feeling remained. She was relieved when Cousin Bella pleaded a headache.

"Feel like a walk, honey?" Clint whispered. "I know you need rest, but—"

"I am fine!" And to prove it, Courtney ran up the stairs two at a time and was back in seconds with a light cape.

Outside, a full moon rode high and serene in a blue-velvet sky, tossing moonbeams with careless aim at the stream leading to Innisfree. How many, many times they had walked like this together. Saying nothing. Then both talking at once—only to grow silent again in understanding.

In the talkative period, Clint told her every detail about the mines. She asked questions and he answered them. But neither made mention of Horace Bellevue. Then Courtney's words tumbled end-over-end and Clint asked questions. But she omitted her visit to the doctor. It was trivial.

They stopped. Clint took her in his arms. And Courtney was sheltered and at peace. Summer would end. The world would sleep—with the promise of something marvelous to come.

And then the beautiful silence was split by Mandy's bloodcurdling scream: "Great day in de mawnin'! Dey dun kilt one 'notha!"

CHAPTER 20
Tumultuous Arrival

From the shadows in the foyer, Courtney stared incredulously at the scene before her. Standing, like carved statues, at the foot of the stairs were three adults, whose backs were to her and Clint. Mandy whose eyes were rolled skyward in horror. A tall man, his outline vaguely familiar. And a stylishly dressed young woman. The fact that they wore hats coupled with suitcases at their feet said they had arrived only moments ago. Something in a small corner of Courtney's mind said that she knew these people; but, in the tumult, the thought was of no consequence.

"Ah dun cou'den stop 'em," Mandy was gasping in an effort to explain. "Dey looks lak angels, but dem white chuld'run's mo' lak li'l black demons—don' lissen—don' mind uh word—don' be carin' 'bout Miz Arabella's headache—"

A crash shook the house. "See whut ah means—de Mansion's gonna be knocked clear offen de foundation!"

The ominous silence that followed was worse than the crash itself. That it portended disaster there could be no doubt. This Courtney knew instinctively although only seconds had passed.

She was right. Down the banisters they slid—two curly-golden-haired cherubs right out of Raphael's painting, except that their wildly waving hands affirmed Mandy's suspicions that they might have come from elsewhere!

"Wide a horse! Wide a horse! Giddyup!" The innocent-faced boy, just inches behind a near-identical little girl (about three, were they?) raised eyes as deeply blue as perfect sapphires to his audience. "This time I'm th' injun and Jonda's the 'merican. When I catch her, I'll scalp her with my bowie knife!"

It was then that Courtney, to her horror, caught sight of Mandy's butcher knife in one chubby fist.

To the little girl, the game suddenly became too real. Her red cheeks flushed and tears spouted from between long wet lashes just as she screamed. "Help me, help! He's wicked—mean—and bad. I hate you, Jordan Grecho —hate you—"

The young woman in the shadows wrung her hands in despair. "Lance, *do* something—" she pleaded helplessly.

Lance! Then the woman must be Vanessa, the twins' mother. Not that it mattered. Here was a crisis. . . .

Courtney and Clint darted ahead of Lance Sterling to rescue the pair from what would have been certain tragedy.

Clint scooped Jordan into his arms, ignoring the lusty protests, and disarmed him. "Look here, young man, butcher knives belong in the kitchen. We *walk* down stairs. And we treat young ladies like ladies. Understand?"

"She's no lady—she's my sisder—and—" the childish voice shook a bit as if he, too, were about to resort to tears, "Jonda's not hurted—just wants 'tention—"

True or false, the wee Goldilocks was getting the attention. Courtney had rescued Jonda from her precarious position on the banister while Clint took care of Jordan.

"Stop crying, darling. Everything is all right—*sh-h-h, sh-h-h.*" Seated cross-legged on the floor, the child's shining head against her breast, Courtney rocked her back and forth until the sobs turned to hiccups.

The boy's frightened eyes sought Clint's. "You're not my boss—are you?" The last phrase came out uncertainly.

Clint gave an able-bodied laugh. "We will talk about that later. Right now, how about shaking hands—and Mandy, do I smell molasses cookies?"

Jordan gave an immediate whoop of excitement. But Jonda remained in Courtney's lap, sucking her thumb uncertainly. "I—we—we bof want our Nandy—"

Not their mother—their nanny. Courtney, still on the floor, cast her eyes upward to meet her sister's. Where on earth had Vanessa been? How had she let these beautiful children become uncivilized little demons?

For a fleeting second the problem at hand shrank. Courtney once again was seeing her older sister as the ravishing beauty she was. Even now, tired from the journey though she must be, Vanessa looked unrumpled. Her fashionable serge traveling suit followed the curves of her body to the white, high-button shoes as if she had been poured into it. The smart beret, matching the light brown of her suit, she had consciously adjusted at an angle to reveal every wave of the dazzlingly golden hair. In a way, she outshone Mother, Courtney thought with the familiar pang. The little air she had, a way of covering any imperfections of character with a sway of her body or the arch of her perfect brows while her gold-tipped lashes lowered slowly to screen the blue of her eyes provocatively. Courtney sighed. No wonder she was the toast of Europe. Why, even the most brandy-tippling old men in Vanessa and Mother's shallow circle used to set down their snifters and make their way to her.

Courtney was aware suddenly of the voices around her. Introductions . . . greetings . . . and here she sat on the floor. . . .

"I'm afraid the children are terribly spoiled—" Vanessa attempted a light laugh.

"They certainly are!" Arabella Kennedy Lovelace's voice rose above the others. She had entered quietly and was now surveying the wreckage around her. "Come here, children!"

Jordan backed against Clint and took hold of his pant leg. "*She*," he said indignantly pointing an accusing finger at his sister, "she doned it! Shame on her!"

"How typical of a man to scold another person when he is frightened." Cousin Bella's voice was not unkind. "Come on, child, I have no plans to eat you—unless, of course, you have been nibbling on my house!"

That brought giggles from both children, who—with gentle nudges from Courtney and Clint—inched shyly toward Arabella Lovelace.

"Are you the wicked witch?" Jonda asked in wonder.

"I *can* be on occasions—but tonight I am your Cousin Bella, providing, of course, this is your mother?"

"I dunno if she is—sometimes she says so—"

Jordan interrupted his sister, "But we don't believe her, do we, sisder? Do you know where our Nandy is?"

Cousin Bella shot Vanessa a withering look. Then, looking down at the children, she smiled. "Well, welcome, Hansel and Gretel. I see you have met your Aunt Courtney and Uncle Clint. Your Uncle Donolar is putting away the carriage. You will meet him tomorrow and he will show you his magic garden—but, for now, it's off to bed for us all."

Mrs. Rueben, with a long-suffering look on her face, offered to show the guests to their quarters. Tardily, the men shook hands. Courtney felt as if she were bringing her own thoughts back from some far-distant country. Where were her manners? She and Vanessa had never been close. But they were sisters and a proper greeting was in order.

She rose and, forcing her leaden feet forward, covered the short distance between them. "It is good to have you here, Vanessa. If we had known, we certainly would have met the train."

"Oh, that dreadful train," Vanessa moaned. "And oh, those dreadful children—I'm afraid they are at their riotous worst at bedtime—you've changed, Courtney."

"I have grown up," Courtney said. "It has been a long time."

The two of them embraced—without affection. As Courtney remembered, the meaningless kiss her sister brushed politely against her cheek—so light that she felt no contact—was the first time Vanessa had ever touched her.

Talk to me, Vanessa. Tell me how I have changed. Tell me you have missed me—that you hope we can grow to know each other—become family.

But Vanessa was adjusting her beret, her eyes following the housekeeper up the stairs. "Coming, Lance?"

Lance! How could she have ignored him—even in all the commotion? Quickly, she turned to extend her hand. Lance took the proffered hand, his luminous eyes lighting up in genuine pleasure. They narrowed slightly as he laid his other hand on hers, then burned like coals of fire. The touch was impersonal enough, but the change in expression told Courtney that his fingers had felt the roughness of her once-smooth hand. He would say nothing, of course, even though the fleeting change in expression questioned her happiness here.

Clint, busy with the twins who had left Cousin Bella's side and were now swinging to his hands, did not notice. "Can you make a whistle, Unkie Clint . . . Can you make a stick horse . . . Will we wide a weal horse . . . May we sleep wif you 'cause we don't have Nandy?"

Lance smiled at Courtney, turning palms up. "I'm afraid I was of little help to their mother. Being a bachelor, you know."

Dear Lance. How quickly he recovered and put her at ease.

"How wise you are, Lance! Most bachelors are experts on bringing up children."

There was a little silence and Courtney could have bitten her tongue. Just who in this room *was* qualified? There was only one parent who, alas, seemed to be the least qualified of all.

Clint had scooped up the twins, one in each arm. "Off to bed with you two. Tomorrow, Jonda and Jordan—"

Jonda slipped a dimpled arm about his neck, her blue eyes drooping as she laid her head against his chest. But Jordan let out a howl of objection. "Hansel and Gwetel!" he corrected.

Later, snuggled against Clint, Courtney whispered, "You were wonderful with Vanessa's children—"

He cut short her praise with a triumphant kiss. "What have I been telling you?" he murmured, drawing her close.

CHAPTER 21
Enlarging Mysteries

Arabella Lovelace, authoritative and commanding in her morning frock of black-and-white shepherd's-check percale, carefully adjusted a button on the cuff before tilting the coffee urn. Mandy had arranged Spode cups on the wicker table in the sun room for the mistress of the Mansion and her two second cousins. Now the mistress was in full command.

Handing a cup to Vanessa, she announced formally that the children had gone to inspect Donolar's garden. Clint, as Courtney knew, had left before the crack of dawn for the mines. And, as Vanessa's hostess, she herself chose to forego making the rounds with her husband. And Lance was painting.

Vanessa kept nodding. But it was obvious that she was not listening, paying attention instead to the lengthy stirring of her coffee although she had taken neither sugar nor cream.

"I trust you slept well?"

Cousin Bella's question caused Vanessa to jump, sloshing the coffee over the rim of the Spode cup. "Not very," she responded. "The children were restless—they have never shared a room with me before—and there were strange noises—"

Cousin Bella chuckled. "Just the old house settling down for the night most likely."

Vanessa frowned. "No, not that, something else, hissing noises like bats." She shuddered. "But I felt better when I heard men's voices."

"Hm-m-m-m—could you tell where they came from? We have no close neighbors. That is, except at Rambling Gate, and the house is unoccupied since Mr. VanKoten and your mother were married. You *did* know of the marriage?"

"Mother and I are out of touch. I *did* hear voices," Vanessa insisted, either to win her point or divert her hostess from the subject of her mother's marriage.

But Cousin Bella was not to be diverted. "I brought down the family Bible, Vanessa. I want you to study it carefully. It is there by the begonia plants."

Vanessa's eyes widened at sight of the enormous book.

"I know all I need to know—Lance has told me about our—uh, poor unfortunate brother—"

Arabella Lovelace bristled. "The only thing unfortunate about the wonderful lad is his having been abandoned by his mother!"

Vanessa, as if a spring had been released, sprang to her feet in something akin to indignation. "Mother had a right to happiness in her own life—" she began hotly, her face flaming with color. Then, just as quickly, the color drained and she sat down with surprising meekness. "I don't know," she said almost inaudibly, "why I am defending her—after what she has done to me—"

"I am sorry to have upset you," Cousin Bella said, making no move to comfort Vanessa. "You see, my dear, I am old-fashioned. I happen to cling to the notion that a mother's love and pride in her children are born with them—no matter what their human condition. Oh, it may be swept out to sea in case of a storm; but the tide should bring it back."

"I shouldn't have come—I knew I shouldn't—but I was helpless—at the mercy of the world—" Vanessa broke off in a flood of tears.

Courtney would have moved forward. But Cousin Bella waved her back. "Nonsense! We are family. You will come to know that I'm a loudmouthed female—so we might as well come to the point. What brings you here and how long do you plan to stay?"

It was a critical question. Cousin Bella's eyes pierced Vanessa's soul. Under their dark scrutiny, Vanessa's personality switched back and forth like a pendulum. One moment she showed signs of nerve-racking anxiety mixed with defiance, like an animal pushed into a corner. The next, she was a pallid, pleading child—younger than Courtney, asking protection.

Now the child, looking much like Jonda, Vanessa whispered tearfully, "There was disaster—I—I had to run away, first from Europe—then from the east—oh, disaster stalks me—"

Then, darling, you should know that you cannot outdistance it, Courtney's heart cried out. *You have to stay and face life.*

But the conversation was between her older sister and an older *and* wiser cousin to them both.

"Running is a cowardly thing, my dear. We face a *real* crisis here. The wheat crop was destroyed, so we have to ration our daily bread. Of course, I am aware that you know nothing of eking a living from the soil, so let me explain that we of the Kennedy Mines are praying the new strikes hold . . . no, I suppose you know nothing—nothing good, that is—of mining either. Just let me assure you that the thought of leaving never occurred to most. We accept the challenge with pride. The idea of running would be repugnant—now, let's look that private disaster of yours in the eye. I guarantee you that there is a cure—"

Vanessa had stopped crying. She looked as if she would rather be back at either of the sites she had fled than here, but she was ready to talk. Bare her soul. Or cast her burden on others?

But, with unfortunate timing, there was a rap at the door. Mandy admitted, of all people, Horace Bellevue. He greeted the trio, his roving eyes appraising Vanessa familiarly.

"Good to see you again, Cousin Vanessa!" (*Again?*) "It was my good fortune to be in your brother's office yesterday afternoon when your sister arrived," he told Courtney with a gleam of satisfaction. Then to Vanessa, "Efraim sends word that your papers will be ready by the end of the week. He knows you are in a rush—but I should like to show you Rambling Gate—"

CHAPTER 22
Vanessa's Mission

Vanessa took Courtney into her confidence the next afternoon. They sat by the creek and, making sure there was no audience, unlaced their shoes, removed garters and stockings, and wriggled their toes in the water. Then they fell silent.

Courtney wondered if Vanessa realized that this was the first sisterly thing the two of them had ever done. It had pleased her to hear Vanessa's giggle. But now she wondered just where her sister's mind had taken her. Entangled in her own problems, she scarcely noticed Courtney. However, it was impossible to mask her emotions. Obviously, Vanessa had put on blinders to cut out the wild beauty around her in order to give full attention to her own plight. She would speak when she was ready.

The sun slipped behind a cloud to cool the air. The cloud passed. The sun redefined its shape and shot fire on the already parched fields behind them. But Courtney failed to notice. She, too, was thinking—thinking back on the early morning.

*   *   *

The crash-banging coming from the room Vanessa and the children occupied spelled trouble even before there was an urgent rap on Courtney's door. "Come—oh, come quickly!" Vanessa cried in near-hysteria.

What on earth were the twins up to now?

Courtney was soon to find out. The large, airy room—now golden with the rising sun—was in wild disorder. Toys were strewn between and underneath the beds. And the pair, still clad in nightshirts, were jumping from tables to chairs in a mad chase.

"They're driving me stark, raving mad—oh, what is *wrong* with Donolar? He caused all this—stop that, Jordan, *this minute!*"

Vanessa, half-crazed, raised her hand as if to strike whichever of the children she could catch. Courtney reached out and restrained her.

Donolar did not start this, Vanessa, she thought sadly. *They are your children. It is you who allowed them to get out of hand.*

But aloud she said, "Well, good morning, Hansel and Gretel! What part of the story are we playing this morning?"

Jonda ran to her and raised a golden-hair-framed tear-stained face, looking for the world like a grieving cherubim. "Hol' me, Auntie Courtney—don' let me get hurted—"

Jordan, his dimpled chin stuck out belligerently and his eyes waging war, rubbed his butter-colored curls with the cuff of a blue sleeve. "Sisder's a sissy—not brave like David what shot the giant with a bow'n arrow—"

Courtney kept a straight face, not daring to correct the error—and set him to making slings and collecting stones which were all too plentiful.

"Who told you the Bible story, darling?"

"Unkie Donny—he knows *lots* of stowies—"

"See? What did I tell you?" Vanessa interrupted.

Courtney put a warning finger to her lips and turned her attention again to Jordan. "Uncle Donny does know a lot of stories he will share—*if* you promise Mother that you will not make games of them without her permission."

"Her's not—"

"Promise, or there will be no more stories!"

The children solemnly promised. But Courtney's mind was on their persistent denial of their mother. It occurred to her then that Vanessa had seen little of them—perhaps almost nothing until the train trip from east to west.

"Pway with us, Auntie Courtney. *You* show us how."

Courtney found little Jonda's request hard to resist. But, since Vanessa obviously was going to do nothing—

"First, let's get this room in order. Then we will see about the rest of the day. There is a box in the closet, Jordan. See if you can handle it."

"I can handle it. I'm a man—Jonda's not!"

"Quite right," Courtney nodded. "But remember what Uncle Clint told you about how to treat ladies?"

"I 'member," Jordan said a bit sheepishly. "I'll let you help, Jonda," and then, as if to preserve his masculine pride, "but I get to lif' the heavy part."

Happily, they set to work. Courtney inhaled deeply and sent a small prayer of thanksgiving winging heavenward.

"You're wonderful with children," Vanessa whispered below the children's chatter. "Both of you are—you and your husband. Even these problem children adore you. Why?"

"We relate well with children," Courtney admitted. "I guess I never wondered why—except that we love them and they know it. But we expect them to obey. And we do not spoil them. It is such a pity—such a waste to let them go untrained—not teaching them self-restraint, finding their talents, and developing them as God intends—"

Courtney stopped. It was heartbreakingly obvious that her sister understood nothing of what she was saying—either about the upbringing of children or her reference to God's plans in their lives. But how could she?

Courtney had learned from the wonderful examples here on the frontier—not in the godless world which Vanessa knew. *Oh, Mother* . . .

A small tug on Courtney's hand brought her back to the present. Two pairs of great blue eyes—so like Donolar's—looked into her face. Crisp curls were damp, and cheeks were flushed like red flames. "We doned it!"

"And I am very proud of you." Courtney stooped to give them each a kiss. "Listen!"

The two stood very still, eyes alight with wonder as there came the beautiful whistle of a mountain quail. "We know—we know—it's Unkie Donny's pwivate signal—us can pway now?"

* * *

The two girls, the dark and the fair, sat among the ferns so long, so still, and so silent that they seemed but a beautiful finishing touch to nature's landscaping. It was the fair one who spoke at last. "I wish I were a good mother," she said wistfully. "No—no, I don't—I wish I were not a mother at all!"

"Oh, Vanessa! How *could* you give voice to such a thought?" There was an unusual ring of sharpness in Courtney's voice. "I am sure their father must have been very proud of them."

"Their father," Vanessa said in a tart voice, "never laid eyes on them!"

There was a pause, then Courtney broke the uneasy silence. "I try to avoid interfering. But you did invite a question with that remark, Vanessa. As a matter of fact, you have left me completely in the dark about whatever 'terrible awful'—as you phrased it—thing brought you here."

"Promise not to be too hard on me—try to understand—"

Courtney nodded. Vanessa waited a moment as if her thoughts were in a whirl. "It all goes back to Mother—"

"That figures."

"She was infatuated with Lord Fredric Grecho—and I meant no harm. I met him—and, well, I—"

Courtney nodded again. "Flirted," she filled in, seeing a vision of Vanessa's great blue eyes provocatively peeping over a feathered fan—a skill their mother employed.

"Maybe—but we fell in love, and Mother could never, never accept his preference—and in a sense she was right, I suppose, but when I learned his purpose, it was too late—do you understand?"

"Not yet. Just let it all out, Vanessa. I have a strange feeling that your story somehow involves me."

How right she was!

Haltingly at first, then with words tumbling out, her sister recounted the strange events that led to heart-break—and possibly death.

Vanessa and Lord Grecho married hastily, Vanessa never questioning his motives. Mother was infuriated and vowed to get even, which she did—tenfold. The nobleman (who was anything but what that title implied) chose the younger woman—the way he would have chosen a brood mare (his lifework being the raising of race horses)—strictly for the purpose of giving him acceptable heirs. Vanessa conceived immediately, but the lord never saw his prizes. He was killed in a race before their birth. In fact ("Oh Courtney, this is the horror of it all!"), there was talk that, regretting his marriage, he grew careless and thus hastened his death.

"Oh, you poor darling," Courtney said sadly when Vanessa paused to get her breath. "But how did Mother—"

"Mother hired a string of lawyers who dug out the awful fact that my husband, if one could call him such, was a bigamist! He had a living wife in France who refused him a divorce—and Mother told all London society that the children were illegitimate!"

Vanessa stopped short at the sight of her sister's face. And then she whimpered, "You promised not to judge—"

Judge? Had there been mention of the word? Judgment belonged to the Lord.

"I have a feeling that the story has not ended, Vanessa."

"Say you are not angry," Vanessa pleaded. Her voice was that of a child.

"I am not angry—why should I be? But I am puzzled as to what I can do, other than offer sympathy."

Vanessa dropped her head. "You are going to hate me—but it is a chance I must take. Yes, there is more—"

Vanessa was in love—*again*. Oh, it was real this time! The only problem being—well—she had not found it within herself to tell him that she had two fatherless children. And oh, she was unable to bear the thought of losing him—

So? Courtney was staring at her older sister now, an awful possibility having occurred to her.

So, if she and Clint would take the children—oh, just for a little while—until after the wedding.

"Vanessa, how can you entertain such a thought? That is no way to start a marriage. It is deception. I have learned the hard way that *any* deception—whether it be a small exaggeration or a withholding of truth is wrong . . . no way to start a marriage—"

"But I have done nothing wrong—circumstances make me no adulteress. And who calls an omission of truth a *lie*?"

"God."

Vanessa cringed. "Then you will not help me?"

"Oh, Vanessa," Courtney murmured with a sagging heart, "let me think—and talk—and *pray*."

CHAPTER 23
A Family Affair

During the next 24 hours Courtney did all three. The thinking brought her no closer to a decision. Her mind's endless rotation only proved, she thought foolishly, that the earth was round . . . moving in circles . . . and, certainly incapable of outrunning disaster, as Cousin Bella had said.

Cousin Bella! Of course, she was the first one to consult. Mansion-in-the-Wild belonged to her.

But Cousin Bella had laryngitis. Fussing and fuming, she lay without a voice, a damp stocking wrapped around her throat. Her high color spoke of fever. Courtney took hot tea to her bedside, kissed the hot, dry forehead affectionately, and tiptoed out just as her cousin dozed. Talk must wait.

Doc George was on his rounds. Clint was at the mines since Brother Jim had expressed a strong desire to check on Lum Birdsey. He seemed to have dropped out of sight—and, with his problem—who knew? There was Lance, of course. Dear, dear Lance. There was nobody with whom she could communicate better. But Lance, having heard the whole story on the trip West, stayed discreetly out of sight. He painted. And he made frequent trips to town. She had neglected him sadly. But this was a family affair.

Surely, the Lord must have heard her unspoken prayer. For, just as Courtney was on the brink of despair, she heard the sound of buggy wheels. Close. They had to be close. Else the dry pine needles would have muffled the

vibration. She sprang from her vigil at the window—
hoping for she knew not what—and, hiking her cotton
skirt above her shoes, bounded down the stairs with
renewed energy. *Efraim.* It had to be Efraim!

It was. And with him was Roberta.

"Oh, I could not be happier to see you—no way could I
be happier!" Courtney cried, embracing them both.

"Why, little sister, I expected no such welcome! That,"
Efraim teased, "must mean the lady is in need of big
brother!" Then, seeing the glisten of unshed tears in the
dark eyes, he sobered. "What is it, darling? Let's go
inside!"

Roberta declined. She needed to check on Rambling
Gate. And no, she did not wish to take the buggy. It was a
beautiful day and she needed the walk.

Efraim made no protest but did tell her to be cautious.

"Of what?" Roberta said flippantly.

Efraim shrugged. If ever Vanessa's dilemma was settled, something had to be done about Efraim's. But not
now.

Courtney led him to the sun room and indicated a
rattan chair. Efraim seemed not to hear, pacing back and
forth as if he, too, were wrestling some problem.

"Where are the twins?"

"With Donolar. They adore him."

Efraim nodded, then stopped in front of where Court
ney sat on the white settee, his legs wide apart to give
him a planted look. "That's good—I guess. Those two are
unaccustomed to being ignored—and Vanessa! Never
mind, let's talk about the children. What is your impres-
sion?"

Courtney laughed. "The same as yours. They are ador-
able, have no idea what obedience means—and gifted
with enchanting smiles which they rightly calculate will
melt hearts of ice."

"They need a firm hand!"

"Indeed, they do—" Courtney paused, the truth dawning. "Sit down, Efraim, please do. Let's stop dancing around the camp fire and talk. You know the whole story, right?"

"Move over a bit," Efraim said. Then, seated beside her, her brother took her hand, stroking the roughened surface. "But are you sure *you* do? These little hands are too busy already—"

"*Efraim!*" The voice belonged to Vanessa. Her eyes were no longer filled with harassment and something in her manner said that her battle was over. She had dressed with unusual care. Her slender body was clad in a walking dress of crimson cashmere with three graduated folds circling the skirt—each piped in black velvet—that stopped just above the ankles. A detail not missed by her brother's eye.

"Isn't the skirt a trifle short, Vanessa—for these parts anyway?"

"Oh darling, don't be stuffy!" Vanessa was Mother all over again today, her own identity having dissolved like her problems. "And I dare you to say my cheeks are rouged. It's the color of the dress," she smiled, touching the porcelain skin of her face. "It does wonders—"

Efraim rose. "I will drop by and see Cousin Bella—then we will talk. Please remain here, Vanessa."

Courtney explained their cousin's malady. Efraim nodded. "Then I will wait until later, going instead for Donolar. Mandy can manage Jordan and Jonda for a time—"

"Why Donolar?" There was a pout in Vanessa's voice.

"Because he is our brother!"

* * *

Donolar entered, holding something behind him. "Flowers are love's truest language." Vanessa did not look up. Donolar handed the rose to Courtney. Efraim's face flushed with anger. Not an ideal atmosphere for resolving a problem which affected them all. Courtney no longer thought of it as a "family affair." They had never been a family. And sadly, they never could be.

"Vanessa," Efraim began. At that inopportune moment there was a jingle of the bells attached to the latchstring. And there stood Horace Bellevue. That explained Vanessa's mode of dress.

"If your sister would like to see Rambling Gate—"

"My sister is staying here!"

CHAPTER 24
The Dark Side of a Mirror

Efraim endeavored to keep the conversation to the point. Did Vanessa feel that a mother should be away from her children? *Sometimes.* Did she feel it was fair to put such a strain on her sister? *Sometimes.* Was it the extended family's responsibility to look after someone else's offspring? *Sometimes.*

"*Sometimes, sometimes!* For goodness sake, Vanessa, have you no other word in your vocabulary?" Efraim exploded when he seemed unable to cope with his sister's vague and irresponsible answers. "This is a serious matter."

A moment's pause made Courtney snap out of absorption in her own thoughts to see Vanessa's eyes focused on the road leading to Rambling Gate. "A penny for your thoughts!" she said, knowing she would catch her off-guard.

Vanessa jumped and colored visibly. Twisting a brilliant ring on her finger, she mumbled something about the scenery (which she had never given eye to). Then, recovering, "I was thinking that the children would be so much better off here—"

Efraim opened his mouth, then closed it. But not before a strange look passed between him and Vanessa—a look which puzzled Courtney. It was as if they shared some secret—unwillingly. What did it mean?

Before she could think further, Efraim turned palms up in a kind of resignation then rose from his chair. "We have never been much of a family, and I regret that deeply. Cousin Bella tells me she has asked you to explore the family Bible, Vanessa, and that you refused. Now, I must insist. And, while you are at it, why not read a few verses? There is such a thing as being a spiritual family—"

"I'll examine it," Vanessa said meekly. But her eyes were still searching the road.

Efraim consulted his pocketwatch. "I think I should check on Roberta." His tone was normal, but there was an underlying note of concern. "Come along with me, Courtney. And Vanessa, I know you will wish to spend as much time with Jonda and Jordan as possible—in case they do remain. Why not take them off Mandy's hands now?"

Courtney, concerned as she was, found it hard to repress a smile. Vanessa was left with no choice.

Donolar refused an invitation to accompany Efraim and Courtney. He, Courtney observed sadly, was babbling senselessly for the first time in ages. "The Brothers—the Brothers—oh Efraim, take some of my butterflies to protect you."

"Efraim, is there something I am missing—something I should know?" Courtney questioned once they were on their way.

"Yes—yes, there is—and, hang it all, I am not at liberty to tell you. I regret that I agreed to this. Forgive me, darling."

"I trust you, Efraim. Whatever you did was right." She slipped her hand into her brother's as they entered the woods where a soft, green gloom was stealing. The ravine was weirdly still as if afraid to echo the laughing of the stream.

Courtney shuddered, asking herself for the millionth time why the place tightened her nerves. "Efraim," she said, her voice sounding hollow in her own ears, "did I imagine it or did you make a point of keeping Vanessa from Horace Bellevue?"

His grip tightening on her hand, Efraim replied, "You did not imagine it, Courtney. Bellevue has been dickering with her to get the children—"

"The children!" Courtney stopped dead still.

"Yes, incredible as it sounds, he offered to keep them should the family refuse—calls himself family, as a matter of fact. Of course, he had a price attached—he's the dark side of our mirror.

Countless questions came to mind. But the conversation was interrupted by a woman's scream.

"Roberta!" Efraim let go of Courtney's hand and sprang forward.

Courtney wanted to call out a warning—against she knew not what, just something sinister. Something which had a million claws and held her when her own feet would have followed her brother's.

Disoriented momentarily, Courtney was tempted to turn back. Although the pine trees hummed contentedly, their gloom changed from green to purple, hinting of approaching twilight; but—

What was that? Courtney held her breath. The sound of her brother's running footsteps had long since died away along the winding trail ahead.

There! There it was again. The sibilant hiss in the heavy underbrush beyond Rambling Gate. Could that have been the sound Vanessa complained of on her first night at the Mansion? Uncannily, it came again. And with it a strange, unidentifiable odor. Fruity. Fermented. Overpowering.

Coming out of her trance, Courtney lifted her skirts and, skillfully avoiding the blackberry brambles, ran as fast as her petticoats would allow. Thank goodness, there was the bridge and the outline of the trail leading to Rambling Gate.

Once across, she stopped—panting and out of breath. Where on earth was Efraim? A sudden movement in the brush behind the great house suggested that he, too, had heard the strange hissing and—connecting it with Roberta's scream—had plunged across the stream without waiting to cross the bridge. But something was wrong. She could sense it. The door was swung wide open and Roberta was nowhere in sight. When it came to poky, dark places Courtney admitted being a coward. But in a crisis—well, a crisis had to be faced. And this hinted of one.

She tiptoed to the door. And what she saw appalled her. Horace Bellevue was holding Roberta in his arms, his hand across her mouth while he peered nervously through the long line of ceiling-high windows overlooking the brush. He must have been alerted by the sound she heard. But now, deciding there was no intruder, he turned his attention to Roberta. His eyes were intent on her, watching her expression, testing her.

"If I remove my hand, will you promise to be quiet?"

A frightened Roberta nodded, while Courtney wondered just what she could or should do. Oh, where was her brother?

Suddenly, there was a change in Horace Bellevue. "Roberta! You are so beautiful—so—" His mouth was close to hers.

At first, Roberta was too astounded to move. Courtney was about to spring forward. Use her nails for claws. Her teeth for fangs. But Roberta had thrust the repulsive man from her violently. He staggered and fell against a table, upsetting a chair with a terrible crash.

"I thought you were my friend—Efraim's friend—a member of his family. I trusted you!" Her voice was filled with contempt.

"He is none of those." Efraim had stepped in from the side door leading to the veranda. "Stand aside, Roberta!"

Still dazed, Roberta did as she was told, just as Efraim's strong hands closed around the other man's throat.

That was when Courtney went into action. "No! No, Efraim! He isn't worth it!" She tugged at his arm.

Pale of face and shaken, Efraim let go. "You're right. Now get out of here, Bellevue—and if ever you return— *get out!*"

CHAPTER 25
"Let the Little Ones Come unto Me!"

Nothing anybody attempted had fazed Vanessa. Once or twice Courtney had felt a flicker of hope in miniature only to have her sister extinguish it. Vanessa's purpose, no matter how cleverly disguised, was like the relentlessness of the summer sun. Well up in the sky now, defying the change of seasons, it burned its brightest, blistering the tardily replanted gardens, baking the earth to pottery, and setting the hindparts of the work teams glistening with sweat.

Well, a decision must be reached. And soon!

"Sweetheart, it is largely up to you," Clint had said tenderly on one of their rare nights together. They had taken an after-dinner stroll beside Donolar's moat which caught and held captive the silvery face of the moon. "I love those children—almost too much to *let* them go. But I have two reservations. I am away too much to be a proper surrogate father, which puts a heavy burden on you. Then, there is the eventual parting—are you up to that?"

"I will do what I have to—"

Clint had broken into her sentence with a kiss. . . .

Efraim had taken a firm stance. Vanessa was no mother at all. He loved the twins and would be only too happy to keep them—if things were different.

What things, Efraim?

Courtney gave no voice to the question. Somehow she knew that her brother and sister had made some sort of compact which he would tell her about if it concerned

117

her—wouldn't he? Courtney had a niggling doubt there but did not express it.

The secret *had* to involve her, Courtney thought—suddenly remembering that matters were made right between Efraim and Roberta. But she would not speak of that to Efraim either. She had promised Roberta that she would not violate the confidence.

"Oh Courtney, I am so ashamed. I—I feel so *unclean!*" Roberta had said brokenly the first time the two girls were together following the dreadful incident at Rambling Gate.

"You were not at fault, dear Roberta," Courtney defended.

Roberta sighed deeply. "In a sense I was. I desperately wanted your brother's attention—"

Courtney laughed. "You got it!"

Roberta visibly relaxed. "Thank you, Courtney—thank you for everything you have done for me here. You helped me to find my self-worth. You showed me how to make the most of my best features which I thought would catch Efraim's eye. When it failed—"

"It did not fail, Roberta."

Roberta gave no indication of hearing. "When he made no overture, I—well, when Horace Bellevue offered to give me a hand at Rambling Gate, I snapped him up in spite of your warnings. I did need help, but—oh, I am so ashamed—I—I wanted to *force* Efraim into a declaration. And, simpleminded as it sounds, I set out to make him jealous."

"Did you tell Efraim this?" Courtney asked quietly.

Roberta blushed. "As much as I dared—without as good as proposing to the man!"

"He cares deeply for you, Roberta. It was written all over him—and I know my brother. He does not play games with young ladies' hearts. Give him time. Right now, he is torturing himself with Vanessa's problems.

And he is trying to decide how to tell Clint about the encounter with his half brother. Efraim has taken his commitment to the Lord very seriously and is wrestling with revealing to Clint just what Horace Bellevue is. Efraim always hopes for change—although he seems to have had his hopes dashed for our sister."

"Oh, those precious twins! I wish—well, never mind. But there is something more I want to tell you, Courtney, about—about Horace Bellevue. Something is going on at Rambling Gate. I sense it. In fact, I *know* it. But he is as slippery as an eel. I was hoping to find out—so my intentions were not all bad."

Roberta was unable to explain further as Efraim entered the sun room where the two girls were talking. Right now, this moment, Courtney would like to inquire of her brother if he suspected anything amiss at Rambling Gate. But that, too, must wait.

"It all seems wrong, Efraim. Vanessa is restless—cross with Jordan and Jonda, which, I must say, is doing nothing to improve their behavior. What shall we tell her?"

"Sooner or later Vanessa is going to have to confront the world outside herself, deal with it, and learn to live in it—" Efraim began. There he paused. "Yet I don't know if she will, darling. Our mother never did. I guess you will just have to decide what is best for our little niece and nephew."

Yes, their niece and nephew. Their flesh and blood. Was there any choice really? And yet the imp of misgiving twisted and turned in Courtney's heart.

Cousin Bella was no help. She kept pointing at her throat. But Courtney suspected that the laryngitis was long since gone. Doc George listened to Vanessa's plight again with twinkling eyes. "You and Clint wanted 12. This could cut the number to 10!" Brother Jim came and prayed with Courtney, then said the children's father was a "bug who ought to be stepped on." Courtney, feeling that she could shake them all out of sheer exasperation, turned to Donolar. He looked perplexed, then overjoyed. With great, expressionless eyes, he said, "Let the little ones come unto me." Mandy and Mrs. Rueben should be consulted. But, driven out of their wits by two "imps" bent on destroying the household, neither of the women was in a mood to be tampered with. Cousin Bella, during her "affliction," had turned running of the household over to Courtney. Consequently, she was compelled to listen to the mumblings and grumblings of the cook and housekeeper. As Courtney understood, Jordan spotted a hornets' nest and stirred it up—literally and figuratively. His method of attack was to supply Jonda with a long stick and send her up a ladder with the weapon.

Fortunately, the children were not stung. But the hornets swarmed in the kitchen window and regrouped—first in Mandy's frizzled braids, stinging as they went (and she did further damage by swatting her head with the mop). "Oh, de pain warn't so bad, but dat Miz Rueben dun claimed ah drove dem hornets up de legs uv her pantaloons."

The result was an icy silence. Only now had it thawed to cool words—and those restricted to bare essentials.

Courtney, turning aside to hide amusement once her fears were allayed, called the twins to her and explained the danger of such escapades. Round-eyed, they listened, then burst into tears.

"We're sorry—bof' of us . . . Will the mean Bruv-ver get us? Will you send us away 'cause we're bad? Are you mad at us? Is God mad—oh, Auntie Courtney—*do we haf' to go?*"

Courtney's heart melted within her. Kneeling, she drew the dimpled children to her, kissing one and then the other. "You are not bad. I am not mad. Nobody is going to harm you. And God loves you! How can I send you away? You are close to Him here!"

And You will have to help me, Lord, her heart implored.

CHAPTER 26
A Time with Lance

Vanessa left the day following with scarcely a backward glance. In a becoming pine-green redingote, with a crimson-fringed parasol shading her white skin from the sun, she sat erectly beside Lance in the family carriage on their way to the train station—a smile of triumph wreathing her lovely mouth.

Courtney was to remember that smile forever. Lance would be back. Vanessa would not.

She wept when Lance returned and told her of Vanessa's departure. "Let go of her, sweet Courtney. Vanessa is as she is—the only way she knows how to be. So desperately dependent on others for happiness—so fair and appealing, but helpless, always in need of a helping hand to rescue her from life's dangers and heartaches. She is very unlike you—but then, we always knew that. She and the Lady Ana depended on each other for emotional security. Strange about life's reversals. Each of them has turned to you."

Courtney nodded. "Mystical and moonstruck, both of them. They have made me feel older than either of them. I pray that always the Lord will give me the strength to rescue them—"

Lance took her hand as the two of them stood in the front parlor. "Dear sweet, caring little Courtney. But what I want is a great helping of happiness for *you*. Nobody deserves it more. I—I have missed you so much—"

Courtney withdrew her hand and touched his lips lightly with her fingertips. His candor and openness were qualities which set Lance Sterling apart. They had said good-bye, but deep inside she knew that Lance had never accepted that. Oh, honor would never allow him to speak of their childhood love again, but she had the responsibility of not reopening the old wound.

"We have had so little time to talk, darl . . . Lance," she said hurriedly. "Donolar is teaching Jordan and Jonda the art of catching minnows. Shall we walk as we talk?"

Together they walked as they had walked so often before—downstream toward the mountain peaks which thrust their snowy peaks high into the heavy towers of cumulus clouds.

"It was a disappointment to me that you were unable to catch this wild beauty with your paintbrush, Lance."

Lance was silent as the stream, lowered by lack of rain, burbled gently past. The wind whined high in the peaks and curled downward to bring a breath of fresh air to the hot afternoon. "I *have* found a subject, Courtney. It is a secret between Donolar and me. But you shall know before I leave."

Courtney stopped and looked into the luminous eyes, reading the same restlessness that was always there. "You are leaving again?"

But of course he would leave. What was there for him here? The long, patrician fingers were created to paint. But never had either of them guessed where his passion for the gift would lead him.

"I was to have done some painting here for Mr. Van-Koten, you know."

"Oh Lance, somebody should have told you about his marriage to my mother!"

"Somebody did," he smiled. And, as they resumed their walk, Lance told her the rest. Mr. VanKoten still wanted his services. He had purchased a large estate, complete with a castle which was a delight to his dear wife, according to a letter written in Efraim's care. The

VanKotens wished original paintings, bearing Lance Sterling's signature, throughout the 24-room French castle.

And Lance would travel to Europe for that?

Well, not solely. There was a great master there under whom Lance had dreamed of studying. Somehow Robert VanKoten had been able to arrange it. Money, a title, brass—these were mediums of exchange anywhere.

"Except here," Courtney said so soberly that Lance laughed. "Here we exchange recipes and homemade soap."

"Just so you are happy." Lance appeared about to say more but checked himself.

They talked about old acquaintances then. Most of those whom they had known during their growing-up years had moved from the New England village.

"And will you be going back, Lance—ever?"

"It is unlikely. I sold Sterling House, you know, to the man Vanessa is to marry."

Courtney was surprised. "She told me nothing. What is he like?"

"I never met him. An attorney took care of the transaction. I only wish that Vanessa had told him everything."

Courtney nodded wordlessly. The shadows were lengthening. It was time to retrace their footsteps. Arabella Lovelace had made a remarkable recovery which meant dinner at six.

Courtney thanked Lance again for his kindness to her family. He waved away her words with an it-was-nothing lift of his hand and turned the conversation to Efraim and Roberta.

"I have never seen a human being more in love than Roberta," Lance said on their way home. And there was a small echo of envy in his voice. "That alone should hasten a proposal. How can Efraim fail to see that her desire is all-consuming? The young lady has changed. Her eyes glisten. The corners of her mouth turn up into a smile when she looks at your brother. One can almost hear her heart break into song."

"I know. Love does that," Courtney said slowly. "Sometimes I feel like suggesting that she shout it out—relieve the pressure on her heart. Oh, what am I saying? No well-bred young lady would do that."

Lance inhaled sharply. "I guess not. And something holds *him* back.

CHAPTER 27
A Letter Edged in Black

❧

After that, Courtney saw little of Lance. He busied himself with the project he and Donolar shared in secret. Sometimes Donolar went along with him, helping to carry palette, easel, brushes, and paints. But, most of the time, he was occupied with the children. Seeing the three of them together warmed Courtney's heart. They spoke the same language that only those who have never crossed over childhood's borders know. Pure. Sweet. Innocent. Inquiring and willing to believe.

Nobody knew how long the children would be at the Mansion. Vanessa's *temporarily* could mean anything. Cousin Bella and Courtney decided that the best temporary quarters would be in the room adjoining Courtney and Clint's master bedroom. The smaller bedroom had belonged to the maid, a young Indian girl, of Columbia's "First Lady," the charming wife of Dr. John McLoughlin. Donolar built bunk beds, much to Jonda and Jordan's delight. And, after the one encounter, Courtney needed mention no more the importance of picking up and putting away toys. Now "Unkie Donny" was making them a tree house, they told Courtney—high, high up, almost to heaven. Its name, of course, was the "Tower of Babel."

Conversation seemed to center around wheat now. Maybe it always had and Courtney was too preoccupied to take note.

"Seems strange," Doc George observed, stroking the full white beard responsible for the children's calling him "Doc Santa." "No shocks of grain curing in preparation for the fall threshing. As a boy I always dreaded the season—all the socket-loosening flailing. Now I would welcome it."

Cousin Bella nodded soberly. "Right you are, George Washington. What I remember most is the feeding of the threshing crews. Such appetites—bigger than those of the circuit riders."

Brother Jim cleared his throat. "Well now, farmers will be getting back to the fields to plant the winter wheat after the first frost—and I see the leaves are taking on a tinge of color. They'll feel better then."

Doc George shook his cloud of white hair doubtfully. "Risky business, wheat. Plant too early and the shoots are apt to get themselves beaten down like this year. Then there are the pesky insects. Lucky we have the *Farmers' Almanac* to plant by. Plant in the right phase of the moon and the seed will germinate properly underground. Of course, there's the geese to consider. One ward can wipe a fellow out."

"But dem's mighty good eatin'!" Mandy licked her lips at remembered goodness. "Y'all dun got yo' shotguns loaded?"

"Worry, worry, worry," Cousin Bella scolded quietly. "Let's put this in the hands of the Lord and trust—no hail, no bugs, no floods or droughts, just one big bountiful harvest."

"Aman!" Mandy affirmed and began planning the details of a banquet. "Sweet taters still in de root cellah, hush puppies, 'n canned ras'berries fo' d'zert 'cuz de flo'ahs a'gittin' low—we dun gotta make do wid co'n meal, Miz Arabella."

"Never mind, Mandy. We don't have the goose yet—"

"And—" Doc George said thoughtfully, "farmers don't have their loans for new seed either. If the bank will float the loans long enough—say, what's this I hear about some mystery man who seems to be offering to stake the farmers and mortgage their homes?"

"Dangerous business," Brother Jim growled, "work of the devil."

Cousin Bella's back stiffened. "*We* will carry the men," she said coldly. "The farmers are not where they want to be any more than miners would take kindly to drowning out digger squirrels from a wheat field! But it is a living. And they need no meddling from outside."

Courtney's heart had gone cold within her. Did they know? Did they suspect? The Shylock among them, of course, was Horace Bellevue. Again she asked herself the source of his income. And again she wished for a time alone with Clint. He had been wonderful to come home as often as he could. But it was neither often enough nor long enough to ease the ache of loneliness she felt. The family had questions. The children surrounded him, telling him of their activities, begging for stories, and, as a final ploy, lengthening their prayers. Their demands did away with Clint and Courtney's walks after dinner when there was so much that needed talking about. Horace Bellevue. Rambling Gate. And yes, if she insisted that her sister be open in all things to her future husband, she must do the same with Clint. She must tell him what the doctor at the fort had said.

Courtney had hoped that these subjects could evolve smoothly, unrushed, naturally . . . that they could talk as they once talked, opening up the private corners of their hearts to each other . . . letting out their dreams. She wanted to hear again her husband's ambitions . . . to draw him out . . . encourage him. And to have him hold her close and tell her that the doctor was wrong. Time together, that was all they needed. Only then could they once more see his "Dream Country" through one another's eyes . . . confess their yearnings . . . make their plans.

With other people around always—no matter how well-meaning—there simply was no time for real communication . . .

Courtney was deep in such thought while sewing a button on Jordan's favorite "towboy shirt" as she sat in the sun room. Suddenly, she felt rather than saw a shadow cross the carpet beside her. And where there was the usual busy noise, there was silence—silence so loud she could hear it.

"Clint! Oh Clint, *darling*!"

She was up and in his arms so fast that Cousin Bella's mending basket spilled its contents into the chair and onto the floor. Clint held her, his heart hammering, his arms trembling. And something told her—she never knew what—that all was not well. She knew even before his shaking fingers handed her the letter edged in black. *Death*.

"Vanessa," she whispered. And, white-faced, Clint nodded.

CHAPTER 28
The Wake

The crepe on the massive front door of the Mansion was black. But Courtney moved in a white haze of confused emotions. And she was to remember only fragments of the sad events after receiving word of her sister's death.

Cousin Bella said that there must be a wake in memory of Vanessa. Just a small wake, since Doc George had yet to remove his community quarantine for large gatherings. Close neighbors brought food—food that Courtney knew they should have kept for themselves. Donolar filled the house with flowers more from ritual than grief. There had been no love between him and his sister. That made Courtney sad. And there had been no love between him and their mother. That made her the more sad. And to think that jealousy had driven a final wedge between Vanessa and Mother—a wedge which now could never be removed—was almost too much to bear. Was it Job who wrote that man's days were short and full of trouble? Short, yes, before the sparks flew upward. How, then, did anyone *dare* deny love . . . the love of God . . . family . . . friends . . . the whole world? God had loved it so much He sacrificed His Son. . . .

Outwardly, Courtney bore up well. But on her knees alone in her bedroom, she wept until her heart was squeezed dry as she poured out her heart to God. "I am unable to comprehend, Lord, the why of these things. I wanted the hatred that has poisoned our family for generations to end—and I tried, Lord—oh, I tried to help. But I praise You, even in my sorrow, that Vanessa and I had this time together. I praise You that Efraim is still here . . . that I have a warm and wonderful husband who understands my loss . . . and that I am a member of the family beneath this roof and Your spiritual family. Give me the wisdom to help these orphaned children . . . to guide them. . . . I am without a roadmap, so hold my hand. And Lord, I never really confessed to You how fractured my world was when I lost that baby which should have been mine—that sweet, broken baby which slipped into the next world without ever knowing this one. And now I do not know if I will ever have another child to fill that gaping hole in my heart . . . no, I do *not* understand, Lord . . . but I can follow without comprehending . . . because I have faith."

People came. People asked questions in hushed tones. How could it have happened? they wondered. Trains were safe now. They did not run off the tracks—did they? How could it have happened, then, that a passenger train plunged into the river, burying every person aboard in a leaden casket?

The night of the wake, Courtney remembered the flickering glow of a hundred candles—each growing shorter as the clocks, their gongs silenced, ticked the night away.

Efraim and Roberta arrived. Efraim embraced Courtney with something akin to a dry sob then sat silently beside her, gently stroking her right hand. Clint squeezed the left, turning the great pearl encircling her ring finger round and round. He, too, seemed to meditate on the celebration of life as well as the natural mourning when the earthly segment of it is finished. That comforted Courtney. Made her forget the burial at sea and brought in its stead a memory of Vanessa's smile. A smile of triumph.

Oh please, Lord, do not allow Brother Jim to remind us that dust we are and to dust we return, Courtney's heart implored.

And God must have heard. Brother Jim gave the solemn occasion a certain dignity and reassurance. In his frock-tail coat, his massive body reflected in countless shadows in the candlelight, he read from 1 Samuel: " . . . 'for man looketh on the outward appearance, but the Lord looketh on the heart' . . . Almighty God, may our sister, Vanessa, have found peace. Amen."

There was food at midnight. But Courtney would have been unable to choke down a bite. She slipped quietly from the parlor and up the stairs to check on the children. Clint followed.

And there on the shadowy landing they stood. "We watched," a wide-eyed Jonda whispered, " 'cause we *know*." And probably they did, Courtney thought sadly—know in that uncanny way children have of understanding when adults do not. The way she and Lance had understood.

"It's for the mean step-muv-ver who wef' us in the woods to get losted," Jordan gloated with a shake of his tousled curls.

"No, darling, no! It was your mother who lost her way."

Someday God would give her the wisdom to explain.

CHAPTER 29
Lessons in Parenting

Courtney was overjoyed when Clint remained at the Mansion for several days. "Oh Clint, I am so glad," she told him gratefully. "I feel helpless, confused—somehow my disconnected thoughts refuse to let me concentrate. There is love . . . there is duty . . . and, oh Clint, I am not exactly sure to whom they belong," she whispered in the privacy of their bedroom.

Clint had pulled her to him gently. "By *they* I am sure you mean the children—"

Courtney clung to him. "See what I mean? I am unable to make sense—to function without you by my side."

"It's the shock, darling. We all feel it. You have tried so hard to resolve your family's problems and thought all was going well until—the tragedy. And what you thought was temporary is now maybe up to the courts—"

"The *courts*! You mean someone could try to take them?"

"We don't know, but Efraim will. Now, sleep my sweet little madonna."

Oh, the blessed relief of stretching her full length on the luxury of the feather mattress . . . having Clint beside her, stroking her hair until she, like the twins, was in the Land of Nod. . . .

Courtney awoke with a start, wondering what had awakened her. The slanting moon peering through the lower window said the hour was late. Careful not to disturb Clint, she tiptoed to the open window and listened.

There! There it was again. The hissing. And yes, there *were* voices. Men's voices. Tomorrow she must tell Clint something was going on at Rambling Gate—something that must be looked into, made right. But it could wait until morning.

She was about to crawl back into bed when another noise brought her upright. A faint whimper and then a moan. The twins had had their baths and, in matching periwinkle nightshirts, were tucked snugly in their beds—utterly exhausted after upsetting Mandy's churn of buttermilk, parading through the stables in horse collars, and being snatched to safety just in time when Jordan climbed the wisteria vine as Romeo and compelled a weeping Juliet to stand on the balustrade of the upstairs gallery. Now they were sleeping, were they not?

The next whimper answered Courtney's question for her. She sprang up so quickly that Clint awakened and together they ran the few steps to the adjoining room. And now there was a wail of terror—Jordan's voice which broke in half at the sound of footsteps.

"Wobbers!" he screeched, awakening his sister. Jonda began to whimper pitifully, "I wan' my Nandy—I hadda bad dweam—*Nan-dy!*"

Courtney dropped on her knees beside the lower bunk where the little girl lay weeping, gathering the tiny bit of humanity to her. Clint lighted a lamp, mounted the two steps to the upper bunk, and scooped Jordan into his arms.

"What," he scolded gently, "are you trying to do—scare your sister to death?"

Jordan's blue eyes were wide and brilliant. "I—I—never meant to scare her. Girls are 'fraid of the dark. It was the dark that scared her—huh, Jonda?"

Jonda, her eyes matching her brother's, were heavy-lidded and she sucked sleepily on one pink thumb. But she managed to nod. "We bof' 'fraid—'fraid you gonna let somebody else mean take us 'way—that's what I dweamed—"

Jordan, in an instant about-face, reached over Clint's shoulder to pat Jonda's curls. "Don' cwy. Unkie Clint's bigger'n him—huh, Unkie Clint? He can't take us—huh, can he?"

"Who?" Courtney asked through dry lips. But even before the child answered, she knew.

"The ole mean Bruv-ver."

Courtney looked helplessly at Clint, feeling her own eyes widen in fear. But Clint was soothing away the children's fears. Nobody was going to bother them. They could live here "happily forever after." And yes, Uncle Clint loved them very, very much. And so did Aunt Courtney.

"And Unkie Donny."

"Uncle Donny to be sure."

And then it was a game Clint had not planned on. Courtney found herself wanting to laugh in near-hysterical relief as Clint was forced to run through every member of the family—including all the horses and Mouser's kittens. What must he be thinking about this unexpected adventure in the caring for children?

"Now," Clint was saying firmly. "No more—let's get you two tucked back in again. Up you go, Jordan, my man!"

Jordan giggled. " 'What big arms you have, Gwandma!' said wittle Wed Widinghood—but (frowning) will you weave the wight on? I don' think God can see in the dark."

"Of course He can," Clint said. "The stars are His lights. But I will leave this little lamp on to light the stars!"

The children were asleep before their golden curls touched their pillows again.

Courtney and Clint crept into bed. "I'm a rag! I can't remember ever being so tired from a 24-hour shift in the mines," Clint groaned as he tucked the light quilt beneath their chins. "So this is what it is like to be a parent?"

"Sure you want to be one?"

"Very sure. Very, *very* sure!"

They laughed together for the first time Courtney could remember. She snuggled closer, marveling at the agony and the ecstasy of being in charge of children with the man she so loved.

CHAPTER 30
Blackmail!

Gradually the tension seeped from Courtney's neck and back like the homeopathic medicine Doc George poured from his assorted bottles for cure of dog bite and flea bite, bee sting and gnat sting, poison oak and poison vetch, blistered feet and gout. It was a beautiful world, after all. Hadn't God created it?

But the people within it were imperfect. And so she must share some of her discoveries and suspicions with Clint. Already he had been away from the mines too long. So it came as no surprise when he told her that on the morrow he must be getting back. On second thought, would she like to ride along today? The outing would do her good. And they could talk.

Courtney accepted the invitation quickly for fear he would change his mind. In moments she had arranged with Cousin Bella to look after the twins as Donolar was accompanying Lance on their secret painting mission. Her riding skirt was fine, Clint said, but she must wear a sunbonnet or a large straw hat. The sun refused to honor the autumnal equinox and seemed determined to set the fallow fields afire.

Courtney chose a burnt-straw-color leghorn sun hat and was grateful for it when the fiery ball in the heavens appeared to have chosen her for its target. What a relief to enter the cool green of the forest. Well, hardly cool, but shaded from the sun, at least.

"What's on your mind, sweetheart—besides the children?" Clint asked when the sun lost its shape beneath the pines.

"So much—*so* much," Courtney said, wiping the perspiration from her face with a dainty handkerchief. Clint laughed and handed her a garden-sized red bandana.

Courtney favored him with a loving smile. "You think of everything. Did you bring along the jerky and ripe apples like we shared for our first picnic so many years ago?"

"Not so many! But no, I didn't, darling. Would that time allowed—"

Time! There was none to waste. Soon they would be reaching the Kennedy Mining village. She began to talk rapidly, her words spilling over one another in her tongue's haste. She began with the strange noises Vanessa had heard on her first night at the Mansion—noises which she and Roberta heard repeated behind Rambling Gate when Efraim halted Horace Bellevue's advances to Roberta—

"*What?*" Clint reined in beneath a giant oak.

Why had she put it like that? But once the words were out, Courtney knew that she must explain. All the while she told the ugly story her dark eyes were focused on Clint's hard-clenched knuckles on the reins. She dared not look into his face.

"And, that is not all, Clint. Darling, I heard the hissing noises again the night Jordan and Jonda were so restless. Something is going on, Clint—I can feel it."

"Why haven't you told me, Courtney?" Clint's voice was low but unaccusing.

"There has been so little time. My days have been so confusing. But I guess the *real* reason is that—forgive me, Clint—I suspect that somehow your brother is involved. Oh, I regret saying that! I should listen to you—"

"Me?" Clint was puzzled. "Who said I trusted him completely?"

"You must or you would never have him in charge at the mines. But what I meant was your saying that most people would rather prejudge a man than get to know him—and I *have* tried!"

Only then did Courtney dare look into her husband's face. There she met what she had feared. Anger. White-hot, seething anger.

"Oh Clint, I beg your forgiveness!" Reining Peaches closer beside him, she reached for his hand, found it, and gripped it hard. She was grateful that he squeezed hers in return.

"You are right in telling me. And I do suspect some things—some of which it is better that I not discuss. Trust me—and be on your guard every minute! I would be unable to bear it if anything happened to you—"

"Nothing is going to happen to me, darling," Courtney promised as they resumed riding. "You see, I must bear 10 more children to make that dozen we planned."

Unaware that she had spoken of the twins as if matters were settled, Courtney was on the verge of telling him about her visit with Doctor Ramsey. But Ahab had seen them from afar and came running.

"Oh Miz Courtney, hon, now if yu' ain't a sight fer sore eyes! We all'uv been lonsome fer the likes uv you—me'n my wife 'n ever' body since they's been no church-goin'!"

The smithy, clad in his greasy leather bib apron, his massive shoulders resembling railroad ties, wiped at his brow with a sooty hand. "Oh, I wist the missus could see yu!"

"She will soon, Ahab. I promise. Brother Jim is talking about resuming the services now since Doc George thinks the strange malady is conquered," Courtney said, raising her voice above the ring of his two anvils in their noisy duet.

Her high-pitched voice alerted Tony Bronson who came from the company store in a dead-run. His "Hallo,

hallo! Oh, praise th' Lord, 'tis th' purty wife of th' bossman hisself!"

The greeting brought the miners and farmers-turned-miners (until the next wheat crop). And Courtney found herself chatting away the time it took Clint to discover that he would be unable to accompany her home, after all. Doc George would be by soon and she could ride along with him.

Courtney did not wait, however. Some sudden, unexplained urgency to get home churned inside her and, once she was alone, she urged Peaches forward—not stopping until they reached the Mansion. "Sorry, girl," she whispered to the sweat-soaked little mare. "You'll feel better after a roll in the pasture."

She looked around for Donolar. He was not in sight, so she unsaddled Peaches herself, feeling a surge of pride in herself. Cousin Bella met her at the door.

"I feel a mite uneasy. Donolar came for the children—wanting them to see the goldenrod beyond the bluff. They were to be right back—Courtney, wait! There was a man who rode by—"

But Courtney did not wait. She ran in the general direction of where Lance usually painted—driven by the same sense of urgency that made it impossible to wait for Doc George.

In the wooded ravine she stopped, feeling a little chill tingle at her fingertips. It was too quiet. Late sunlight bronzed the mossy waterwheel making it stand out in bold relief against the gloom of the woods. Again the feeling of being watched—that she must run. And she did.

How foolish she was, she thought moments later. A little beyond, on a ledge above the dozing shallows of the once-busy stream, stood a pair of laughing cherubs, dangling strings with hunks of Mandy's "lard fat" knotted to the ends into the water. Of course—Donolar was teaching them the art of catching crawfish!

She was about to call out to them in warning so Lance could cover the canvas on which his secret was painted, when a twig snapped near her. Cautiously, she turned.

And there, watching the children, was Horace Bellevue! The horrible word "kidnapping" came to her mind unbidden—although what he would want with her sister's children she was unable to imagine. The fact that Vanessa had given him an audience, just as Mother had before her, left Courtney unnerved. And now that she was gone, who knew? With a thudding heart, she recalled that Efraim had said this man offered to take Jordan and Jonda—for a price! And, on the heels of that thought, came the memory of Efraim's handling some papers for their sister.

She must get to the children. Unnoticed if possible.

Too late. Horace Bellevue must have sensed her presence. He was by her side in what seemed but a single stride.

"Cousin—"

Courtney drew back in disgust. "What are you doing here? I thought my brother made it perfectly clear—"

"Your brother," he sneered, "is not in a position to dictate. *I* am!"

Horace Bellevue's small eyes were cool and calculating. Testing the water. "Those kids may be my collateral—unless—"

"Those *children* are not anybody's collateral!" Courtney snapped, hoping that he did not hear the hammering of her heart.

"Let's see—we might make a deal. What is it worth to you if I keep my mouth shut about their background, forget the papers—"

Blackmail! Blindly, she fled toward Jordan and Jonda.

CHAPTER 31
Legacy in Dispute

Efraim registered no surprise when Courtney related the hateful incident. He clamped his lips tightly together and his face was grim. He was silent for so long that Courtney spoke again.

"It is not true, is it, Efraim? Horace Bellevue has no claim? He probably is trying to frighten me—but why?"

The two of them had been sitting in the sun room; but Efraim was standing now. How tall her big brother was. How protective. But his colorless face told her that there were some things in life over which he had no power.

"I am concerned, Courtney. Our sister was unstable at best and, try as I would, I was unable to keep her apart from Clint's half brother. She seemed fascinated—as if he cast some sort of spell."

"Horace Bellevue! I find him despicable. What on earth did she see in the man—and what has he to do—?"

"The family name influenced Vanessa, I think. Anybody bearing the name of Bellevue has to be a thoroughbred. That and her determination to get the children off her hands at any cost."

"Cost, Efraim?" Courtney's eyes widened in shock.

Efraim stopped pacing and stood in front of her, his right hand reaching into his vest pocket. "Vanessa cajoled me into something I wanted no part in—insisted that I prepare some papers—regarding your having custody of Jordan and Jonda."

"Custody? But the arrangement was only temporary," Courtney said in a small voice. "Help me understand.

Was it that Vanessa had some sort of premonition? Oh, how dreadful!"

"Steady, darling, I am sorry I had any part in this sordid affair." Efraim's voice was filled with self-accusation as he fingered the long envelope. "I will speak no ill of the dead—and certainly not of our sister, whom we both loved in spite of her weaknesses. But neither will I have you led astray by some notion that can break your heart. Vanessa," he went on grimly, "had no premonition, Courtney. She simply had no intention of coming back for the children."

"You mean—" Courtney's mouth was cotton-dry, refusing to give voice to words.

Efraim dropped the envelope in her lap. "Read this."

Eyes blurred with tears, Courtney tried to make out their sister's message. "I, being of sound mind, do hereby will and bequeath . . ."

The sum of money was large. Hush money, Efraim told her gently. Money paid by the real wife of the twins' father in return for her silence. Money for the support of the children (or was it to entice Courtney into caring for them?). *Money!* Oh, how she hated the word. How many hearts had been broken in the Bellevue-Glamora family by the love of it?

Courtney forced her mind back to the letter signed by Vanessa and witnessed by Efraim. Her body had gone rigid and an uncontrollable shiver traveled the length of her spine.

"Why did you agree to this, Efraim?" she whispered. "How could you be sure I would consent to this—without Clint's permission. *Why?*"

Efraim dropped on his knees beside her, grasping her shaking hands. "I am sorry, my darling—so sorry. But I was sworn to secrecy and I was afraid—yes, men know the taste of fear sometimes, too—afraid that she would carry through with her threat. In fact, she did in a sense. At least, there is that possibility."

Courtney was stroking her brother's hand absently. She could forgive him anything. And, as yet, there was nothing to forgive. Memory came in an overwhelming tide. He *had* tried to allude to this and she had told him that whatever he did was right.

But now a new terror tore at her heart. She shivered and murmured brokenly. "It reads like something in a book—a very bad book—and I am afraid to turn the page. What—what do you mean, her threat—and your fear of it? Oh Efraim, not—"

Courtney stopped in horror. And Efraim nodded.

"Horace Bellevue claims to have a similar letter bearing a prior date."

CHAPTER 32
New Evidence

Cousin Bella, Doc George, and Brother Jim each reacted strongly when Courtney reported Horace Bellevue's plot. The four of them sat in the backyard, fanning themselves against the late September heat. Brother Jim had resumed some of his house calls since, as far as he could tell, the situation at the mines was under control. Certainly, he declared, his flock was in need of some shepherding. If one could believe the reports of mischief reaching his sharp ears. That was good, the doctor said with a merry twinkle. 'Twould allow him to curtail some of his own calls since danger of spreading the strange disease seemed history. What these people needed was some "churching," sure enough. Cousin Bella kept nodding and fanning—

Until Courtney told her story.

"You mean," Arabella Kennedy Lovelace almost bolted from the garden bench, disturbing the mint bed— the only plant to have survived the heat—"that traitor thinks he can take those children without my consent?"

Doc George, accustomed to soothing feverish patients, attempted to make use of his bedside manner. "Now, now, Arabella, control yourself—"

"How could you defend him, George Washington? I am surprised at you. Why—why, that *Benedict Arnold!*"

The doctor had no chance to reply. Brother Jim had jumped into the ring. In order to gain full attention, with clenched fists he cleared his throat with such a rumble it brought tears to his eyes.

He had it.

"There comes a time when justice must be served. That sniveling, bantamweight pip-squeak has no idea of the wrath of the Lord!"

"Horace Bellevue is a blob of protoplasm, true," Doc George said, "but, Big Jimbo, best we watch our step. He is devious enough to do harm to the children."

"Let him try!" Brother Jim roared. "We have tried to show him the way of the righteous—but there's simply no need in fertilizing a dead tree!"

Cousin Bella stopped fanning. "Oh, my poor babies— little lower than the angels—"

Frightening as the situation was, Courtney found herself tempted to smile at her Cousin Bella's application of the creation Scripture to Jordan and Jonda.

Now everybody was talking at once—and moving as they talked. Where were the twins? They must be guarded every minute of the day. And where was Horace Bellevue? Somebody had to keep a watchful eye on him. Clint! Clint might be in need of a helping hand at the mines.

The men left posthaste. Trust Cousin Bella to alert Mandy and Mrs. Rueben. None of them trusted Horace Bellevue anyway. But Courtney chose to speak with Donolar herself as he was the one with whom the twins spent most of their time.

"Come inside, you three," Courtney said breathlessly when she found the trio searching for bullfrogs among the cattails beside Donolar's moat.

Jordan—tired, sleepy, and out-of-sorts—protested with a lusty yell. "We have'n found a fwog yet. We don' wanna go in—huh, Jonda?"

Donolar's great eyes sought Courtney's in perplexity. Obviously, this was his first glimpse of Jordan's other side. And Jordan, with the intuitive awareness that children possess, was sure of his advantage. Scream and you got your way.

"That is a lot of noise, Jordan," Courtney said. "I am sure you are shocking Donolar. He thinks of you as a big boy."

Jordan turned exquisite blue eyes on his aunt. Here was a strange adult. She was unimpressed by his tantrum. Then his howls stopped and his golden head dropped in embarrassment.

"Did I shock you, Unkie Donny? I sowry. Oh, Aunt Courtney, am I a mean wittle boy?" Jordan ran to hide his angelic face in her long gingham skirt. "Do you still wuv me?"

"You are *not* a bad boy—just thoughtless. We love you very, very much—too much to allow you to behave like a brat!" She softened the word with a gentle smile and smoothed the damp curls from his hot forehead.

Jonda, standing aside sucking her thumb, had remained silent. Now she rushed to Courtney and burst into tears. "I wanna be wuved, too."

"And you are, darling—so much, so very, very much."

"And we can pway with Unkie Donny?"

"Only if you follow the rules. Now, inside, all of you!"

* * *

Returning, Courtney heard the disturbed voices in the foyer before she was halfway up the front walk of the Mansion. A man's voice blended with Cousin Bella's. The voice was vaguely familiar.

"Oh, Miz Arabella, what're we a-gonna do? I know I made a mistake, but whut wuz I s'posed t'do? Th' bank was foreclosin' 'n I did'n wanta have the Widder losin' her cattle 'cause uv me—"

The Widder. Of course. The voice belonged to Josh Thorson who, widowed and left with a destitute family, had married the Widow Roundtree. But what was the cause of his agitation?

She was soon to find out. Cousin Bella motioned her into the parlor. "You remember Josh Thorson, Courtney."

Courtney extended her hand. "Of course, although this is the first time we have met since the terrible hailstorm."

"Whut took my Della," the man said sadly. "I 'pologize fer not gittin' here sooner—sad news 'bout your sister 'n all."

Courtney accepted his awkward condolences. "And what is the problem at hand? Is there something I can do?"

"Oh, Miz Courtney, if y'kin git the bossman t'reason with his brother maybe. He offered me a loan—demanded a mortgage 'n now is a-gonna take the Widder's house—all 'cause uv me—"

Was Clint so blind about Horace Bellevue? Courtney wondered. But it was Josh Thorson who spoke again. "He's been fired—'n disappeared liken Lum Birdsey—"

CHAPTER 33
Hiram Oakley

It was true. Horace Bellevue was gone. He had vanished into thin air just like the well-meaning, but misguided little shadow of a man called Lum Birdsey who was unable to "let White Lightning be," according to Brother Jim. Courtney *must* see Efraim and Clint.

Hiram Oakley, a leggy man with a potbelly that put so much stress on his spine that it swayed in like a horse forced to carry too great a load, had a beak nose and darting eyes that never rested behind his spectacles. He was as sharp as a briar, Efraim said, and as crooked as a barrel of blacksnakes, according to Cousin Bella. His office was a small storehouse where shipments of staple groceries were stored at one time. The furnishings were simple—a flour barrel for a desk and whiskey kegs for chairs. He kissed babies, Doc George said, and flattered their mothers while robbing the man of the house blind. Oh, not in a way that was punishable by law. Far more devious. Hiram Oakley was a lawyer. The lawyer who had handled the affairs of Horace Bellevue.

Practicing just across the alley from Efraim, Hiram Oakley had watched every move that went on apparently. And, were there such a thing as a listening device, he would have made use of it, Efraim said. It was uncanny how the man descended like a vulture on every client who was in need; and, acting on behalf of Horace Bellevue, declared that a mortgage on their property was the way to outwit the banks. For no, Josh Thorson was not the only one who had been suckered in, Brother Jim reported. One by one, like a plague, he visited upon every debtor. His tongue, like his sparse hair, was well-oiled. It was far better, he pointed out in greased tones, that the men surrender their homes, mineral rights, and all other claims thereto, than to be dragged into the courts. Convicted. Put in jail.

The day Courtney saw him, he was wearing a broad-brimmed beaver hat that made her wonder just what the temperature was beneath it. When he tipped it to her, she saw the beads of perspiration beneath the strands of plastered-down hair which, unable to decide on color, made use of them all, mixing brown, sandy-red, and gray.

"Howdy do, Mrs. Desmond," he said, dodging a stray dog and all but holding the seat of his pants. "I suppose you are on your way to visit with that brilliant-minded brother of yours."

It was really none of the man's business. But Courtney nodded in greeting and hoped to look as if she were not hurrying as she tried to continue across the street. A wagon, driven by a man who did not see her, rumbled by to block her passage. Dun-colored dust swirled up in blinding columns.

Hiram Oakley seized the advantage. "We have not been formally introduced, but I think we know of one another."

That part was true! "Then you will know that I have nothing to discuss with you. May I pass, please?"

The man with the wagon was tethering his team. The dust eddies had settled. And now he was recognizable. John Laughten! Some inner instinct told Courtney that Cara's husband was on his way to see the man before her. She prayed silently that he had not fallen for this man's devilish scheme to steal the entire valley for himself and Horace Bellevue.

John advanced toward them. But the lawyer had not spotted him. "I am sure you recognize that your brother and I are on opposing sides. It is essential that I protect the best interests of my client—and I *do* know how to collect delinquent accounts—"

"I am sure you do! Hello, John. I wonder if you will be so kind as to accompany me to my brother's office. There are *stray dogs* around—" Courtney emphasized the words and looked directly at Hiram Oakley. He had the grace to color and shift his restless eyes to the dirt at his feet. But he did not stop talking. "But remember your appointment, Laughten!"

"Oh John, please tell me that you have signed no papers with this man," she whispered as they hurried away.

John Laughten cleared his throat. "What—what *kin* I do, Miz Courtney? A jailbird's no good to his fam'ly. I ain't signed—but th' papers is ready—"

"Oh, thank the Lord!" she said as Efraim's door swung open.

"Thank *you*, Courtney!" Efraim said heartily. (*What for, Efraim?*) "When you finish shopping, I will ride to the mines with you."

CHAPTER 34

Rendezvous

At the mines Courtney waited while her brother went in search of Clint. He checked first at the Company Store. Tony Bronson, leaning back on two legs of his chair and flailing the air with his leg, sprang to his feet and, literally leaping the vinegar barrels, landed on his feet like a cat in front of Efraim. Yessir, he would fetch th' bossman—makin' haste. No sir, not uh word to nobody—the storekeeper promised—he'd jest bring th' bossman t'th' grove 'way from pryin' eyes.

Mr. Bronson was as good as his word. Clint joined Courtney before Efraim was back. He found them in a tender embrace which tightened as if neither would ever let go again.

Tactfully, he cleared his throat. "Talk about being one in the flesh—I have yet to see you two standing apart!"

There was no denying the twinge of envy in his voice. If only Efraim could know such happiness—

But there was talking to be done—and fast. Clint, still holding Courtney to him and twirling a forefinger through her heavy hair, made the conversation easier. Brother Jim had told him all about Horace Bellevue's schemes to gain title to the valley land. And yes, he said (looking positively dagger-eyed momentarily), about the threat of blackmail to get the children.

"It is true that you fired him?" Efraim asked.

"Quite true! Actually, that was before all this came up. He had been abusive to the men—and there was evidence of his bringing some woman here for lodging. But he kept up the pretext of being in my employ and I let it pass. Rumor had it that he was on the take—and, wisely or otherwise, I quietly did some observing. It all adds up—"

"You knew he had disappeared?"

Clint frowned. "Yes, and that concerns me—you know, wondering what he's up to—"

Efraim reached up to pluck a pine needle and chewed on it before replying. "Actually, that's in our favor. My *un*worthy colleague can do nothing by way of foreclosure with his client hiding out. And, with your permission, Clint, I am appointing myself defending attorney for your men—naming the defendant as Kennedy Mining Corporation. I have spoken with the bank president and sort of stalled him off. He is impressed that the mines are in the black and has been around long enough to know that next year's wheat crop is apt to be the better for letting the land lie fallow this year. As a matter of fact," Efraim inhaled deeply, "I took the liberty of depositing enough with his bank to satisfy the mortgages—temporarily—"

"Oh Efraim!" Courtney whispered with tears in her eyes.

Efraim dismissed the matter with a characteristic wave of his hand. "All in the family."

Clint's next question concerned the children—their safety and their future. "As a matter of fact, who is with them now?"

Courtney laughed. "Cousin Bella, Donolar, Mrs. Rueben, and Mandy—equipped with buggy whips, mop buckets, and rolling pins! They are safer than we are."

Clint relaxed. "Take good care—*good* care—they are the start of the dozen the Desmonds plan. Right, darling?" He squeezed Courtney's hand.

Oh Clint—Clint, my darling—they may be the ONLY ones.

But possible barrenness was something she must discuss with her husband in private. And besides, God had the last word. Stranger things had happened in the Bible.

There was a sound of voices. Another load was coming up from the gaping mouth of one of the mines. The conversation must end. The men talked hurriedly. Efraim was investigating the background of Hiram Oakley. The man claimed to have come from Seattle, but so far there was no trace of his past there. There was a rumor that bounty hunters were on his trail. He had two men checking out the whereabouts of Horace Bellevue, too, as well as Lum Birdsey. Strange, wasn't it?

Very strange. Would Efraim like to bring Roberta out to the Mansion until things settled? Efraim was about to ask permission, he said.

And all too soon Clint was raining little kisses on the part of Courtney's hair. "My little madonna," he whispered—and was gone.

CHAPTER 35
"Another Spring"

Nature, always extravagant with her paintbrush in the Columbia Country, was downright lavish this autumn. October came with a hot-breathed burst of glory. Everything burned golden. At first, not a leaf stirred. Then, on the day Roberta moved into the room Vanessa had occupied, blessedly a silver mist, so typical of Washington, draped the valley and cooled the parched air. By morning, it was raining.

Courtney helped Roberta unpack her few belongings.

"I brought very little," Roberta said with a wistful smile. "I am hoping that all this nasty business will be settled soon and—in the meantime—I am to stay away from Rambling Gate—and hope—"

"Efraim will be so lonely he will be unable to do without you," Courtney laughed.

Roberta sighed. "Yes. That is my prayer—I *do* pray, you know."

Courtney hung a stylish federal-gold-trimmed jumper suit in the closet. "I am glad, Roberta."

"So far no answer."

"God has His own time system. Avoid setting a deadline."

Roberta took a lace-covered corset from her barrel-top trunk. Courtney gasped at the number of staves nipping in at the waist. "My word, Ro! If Efraim proposed, you would be unable to gasp out a 'yes' in that garment."

The girls giggled then sat cross-legged on the bed for a long talk. All she heard was wheat, wheat, *wheat*, Roberta said. Was that all the farmers talked about? This depended on the wheat. That depended on the wheat. *Everything* depended on the wheat. It was their living, Courtney explained. Their living and something else. Farmers were a proud lot. They saw mining as a form of charity . . . oh, they were grateful . . . but . . .

"Listen!" Courtney interrupted. "Canadian honkers!"

Both girls ran to the window to watch the early-starting arrow of geese wedging the gray sky, winging their way south. Their cries of remembered frost touched Courtney's heart.

"There! That is God's first signal, Ro. I marvel at the instincts He gives the feathered creatures. And, if we watch, we can read His handwriting to us. Most likely tonight will be cold after the rain. Then farmers, like those honkers, will hear His forecast of frost." She pointed up and down the barren rows in the only field near the Mansion. "Then you will see farmers dragging out bags of seed they saved from last year's crop, the wheat we would have ground into flour. You did know that we are scraping the bottom of the barrel—literally?"

"Oh, I forgot to tell Efraim—a shipment of flour came—sacks and sacks!"

* * *

The rain kept up. Lance moved inside to complete his painting, calling the turret on the east wing his "ivory tower."

"I suppose Roberta has told you that her father wanted some sketches from the area around Rambling Gate—or maybe she was unaware. My other project is finished. I will be leaving soon."

Courtney and Lance were having coffee together in Mandy's bright kitchen where the monstrous wood stove drove away the dampness and handed out ginger cookies almost as fast as she and Lance could devour them. There had been so few baked goods of late. But news of the shipment of flour had prompted the cook to reach into her bin for a handful she had been hoarding.

Nibbling on a cookie, Courtney was silent until Lance laughingly waved a hand before her face. "Yoo-hoo! I'm here—remember me?"

"I am sorry, Lance," Courtney said without smiling. "I was wondering if you saw or heard anything irregular around the premises of the property."

"Irregular?" Lance frowned as if the word had no meaning. "I'm afraid I would not notice—since I hardly know what is *regular*. Is there a problem?"

Dear Lance. Of course, he would take no note of the hissing sounds and the fruity odors. As an artist, he lived in the world of sight—closing away all of the other senses. He saw the magenta of the sunset and the green in the clinched fists of unopened buds. He saw rainbows in the rain. But he did not love the world. He only loved its color.

She would miss him when he was gone. . . .

*   *   *

A mass of cold air blew in to block the rain. There was a definite feel of frost in the air. But in the great Mansion there was a sense of excitement. Efraim had come to spend the night and tomorrow, after church, he and Roberta would be returning to the city. That alone called for a celebration, Cousin Bella said, since it represented an easing of tension. That cockroach called Horace Bellevue must have taken his disease-spreading presence elsewhere. He was undoubtedly the one who started the typhus here.

"Typhoid, Arabella," Doc George corrected, a Santa-like smile fattening his rosy cheeks and crinkling his eyes. "But, by whatever name, the fact that we have brought the sickness to a standstill is cause for merriment."

"Right, George Washington," his wife, unabashed, affirmed. "And Brother Jim will be joining us for dinner. He is notifying the congregation that there will be church tomorrow!"

Lance, coming into the parlor to ask Doc George a favor, paused at the door. "Pardon the intrusion—I seem to have run out of turpentine and my hands are less than presentable."

Doc George went for his black satchel and Cousin Bella offered Lance a cup of tea. He refused, thanked her, then hesitantly inquired if he might ask a favor.

"Why, Lance Sterling!" Cousin Bella exclaimed in mock shock. "You surprise me. So bold with that paintbrush and so shy of tongue. Ask away. You are our guest."

"For only a short while. And then, sadly, I must leave your pleasant company. Donolar and I beg your permission to unveil our work this evening."

Another cause for rejoicing, someone said.

But Courtney, smiling secretly, was remembering that Clint would be home tonight. Even with Roberta for company, a week away from her husband was much longer than seven days!

Courtney and Roberta, giggling like two schoolgirls, did one another's hair for the evening. Roberta, corseted with Courtney's help, admired her hourglass figure shown off to such an advantage in the simple princess-line apricot-toned wool gown. The color brought out the amber in her eyes and, yes, they decided, the bangs beneath her crown of braided hair were becoming. Roberta insisted that Courtney experiment with the style of her own hair. But Courtney declined. Clint liked her hair, with its simple middle-part, left swinging to her shoulders. No bangs. But the dress was something else. Roberta gasped when Courtney held up the nasturtium-colored dress Clint had hired the French dressmaker to fashion for her on their honeymoon. With a corset . . .

"I think I can get by without one," Courtney said. "Maybe just a camisole and the petticoats. For some reason those foundation garments make me miserable."

Wiping the smiles from their faces, the two young ladies left Roberta's room and entered the dining room just as the grandfather clock struck six and, tardily, the cuckoo clock replied.

The men rose gallantly. There was a little flurry of conversation during the seating—a flurry that caused Courtney to miss the fact that, for the first time, there were two special chairs, piled high with pillows, at the table. She was engrossed first in watching the earth and sky mellow through the long glass windows over which Mandy had forgotten to draw the damask drapes. And then she was watching herself reflected in the blue lakes of her husband's eyes. Why did she think of it just now—the saying that it was a husband's responsibility to build the house and a wife's to build the marriage? Had she succeeded in his eyes . . . did that include the children she had not given?

Courtney reached and took Clint's hand beneath the snowy linen tablecloth. A little meteor of happiness exploded inside her, short-lived but bright-burning in its dying. Letting her see the poignant scene before her in impressionistic art . . . a soft blur of candlelight reflecting on heirloom silver . . . Donolar's centerpiece of yellow chrysanthemums—gold nuggets in the candle-light—the flowers he had potted and moved inside his cabin for a special occasion . . . and the glow of the beloved faces around her. Of course, meteors burn out, leaving holes of darkness in the sky. And somewhere in that blackness lay an uncertain future. But for now . . .

Ponderings were cut short. Brother Jim was praying for those at the table, tomorrow's church service,
next spring's wheat crop, and asking that the Lord deal
mightily with those wayward ones who plotted evil even
if it meant striking them down "with an acute attack of
brain shock!" *Amens* followed. And then at the far end of
the table came a distinct duet of "Hey, man!"

Jordan and Jonda! Already in their pink- and blue-
striped pajamas topped by heavy white bibs, the golden-
haired pair sat with eyes as wide and innocent as purple
pansies. Who had brought about this miracle? The whole
family, undoubtedly, Courtney realized with a lump in
her throat.

"Donolar!"

At Cousin Bella's command, Donolar said without a
hint of a stutter, "Hansel and Gretel will say the Scripture. You first, Hansel—you're the boy."

"Fo' God so wuved the wo'ld . . ." Jordan paused for
Jonda.

"He gave He only fo'gotten Son . . ."

"That who-so-evah wuv 'm should not—uh—
pe-wish . . ."

"But have eveh-wasstin' wife!"

This was their first public appearance. And in the
unpredictable way of children, they promptly burst into
tears and—scooting off their mountain of pillows—ran
to Courtney and Clint.

There was not a dry eye in the room as Courtney
gathered little Jonda close, kissing the tousled curls,
and Clint pulled Jordan onto his knee and praised him
highly. Neither was there a look of amusement in the
faces of those at the table. And for a split second Courtney drew a comparison from incidents she had thought
forgotten—the brittle laughter of adults at children's
stumblings in the world in which she, Efraim, and

Vanessa had grown up. Even their mother's attempt at brilliance and wit to draw attention from them and to herself. *Oh Mother, what you missed!*

The children had had supper, Mandy said. So, while Doc George carved the goose "sighted dangerously near the granary" Clint and Courtney put them to bed. Today these same children had driven Mandy crazy playing hound and fox and, alas, knocking her last jar of naseberry jam from the cook table. Tonight they were weeping angels—if angels wept. Courtney wondered.

There was so much to say after the twins slept—which was immediately. But the big event was yet to come (not that it could outshine this one). So best hurry. But not before Clint said in awe that he never guessed parenthood could be so wonderful.

It was an emotional moment when Lance and Donolar stood beside the easel and undraped the canvas from the mysterious painting. And whatever the imaginings of the onlookers, nobody possibly could have foreseen the majesty of the exhibition.

Courtney, so close to tears anyway, gave way to her emotions completely at the sunlit scene Lance had managed to communicate in oil. Such glory she had never seen as the giant tree in burning gold splendor. There was a symbolism here—something Lance wanted to leave with them—but it evaded her until her misty eyes cleared enough to see the superimposed lettering over the autumn-bright leaves. And then Donolar was reading his very own poem:

> The hawthorn bloomed too early,
> In Easter-bright bouquet—
> The pinks and whites of April,
> But petals blew away.
> And now it is November
> And near is winter's sting

But hawthorns in the hollow
Bloom in Another Spring . . .

Another Spring. Another chance to dream again . . .
another resurrection . . . and Donolar, the "strange one,"
had seen it in the hawthorn with Lance, who dared to
dream.

CHAPTER 36

"Come Home, Come Home"

The Church-in-the-Wildwood was smaller and shabbier than Courtney remembered. But it was home. And it was good to be back! The air was mild after a cold night and Ahab had laid a fire in the potbellied stove that dominated the front of the room. The stove was an ugly creature—ugly and temperamental. At times its metal sides were red-hot while at others it sulked and belched out smoke that kept the ladies dabbing at their eyes. The logical place for the beast, Cousin Bella declared, was at the back so the congregation could catch a glimpse of the pastor. But it was the pastor himself who thought otherwise. "And have everybody warming the back pews? Oh no, my message is not for empty seats—it's aimed at mankind, and them having ears let 'em hear!"

Among those occupying the front seats today were the Lovelaces, the Desmonds, Efraim, and Roberta. Roberta looked especially lovely, Courtney thought, with the black zephyr yarn fascinator framing her ivory face. She looked at peace as if some momentous decision had been reached. And yet, there was a kind of vulnerability about her, too.

It had been a somewhat strange morning anyway. Donolar, who had never missed church, begged permission of Cousin Bella to be allowed to remain at home with Lance. Lance was leaving tomorrow and the two of them wanted to find the exact right place to hang the painting. Cousin Bella consented reluctantly. After all, the child asked so little . . . and hanging a picture was not labor exactly. Mandy kept nodding. " 'Twould be like unto li'l Jonda's ironin' doll clothes—why, de good Lawd dun knows dat chile's iron ain't hot."

Then, Mandy and Mrs. Rueben had insisted on occupying a back pew. True, the twins most likely would be as quiet as church mice. Still and all, just in case one or the other decided to scream "Fire!" and start a riot . . .

Courtney smiled down at the children, pride filling her heart. Seated between her and Clint, they scarcely seemed to be breathing. Their matching navy-blue sailor suits were unrumpled and every curl was in place. She caught Clint's eye above their heads and they shared an I-love-you smile just as the pitch pipe sounded for the first hymn.

Interrupted, the men broke from their outside clusters to join families inside. Their prayers had been answered, they were saying. Yes, for sure, there *had* been light frost in the low-lying areas. The wind was rising—apt to bring sustained cold. Better get sowing, so the seeds could be germinating before the big freeze locked them in until spring. Yes, it would be right nice if man had machines to do the job. All that dropping the kernels by hand then kneeling to cover them sure as shootin' got to the prayer bones . . . but not as hard on a feller as that nerve-raveling watching afterwards . . . watching for grub worms . . . blackbirds . . . geese. Yeah, better be at it tomorrow. Everything depended on the wheat. . . .

Brother Jim stomped to the pulpit and, without hesitation, tore off his removable collar. His red face prompted one of the men to turn the damper down on the stove and pry a window open, letting in a brisk breeze heavy with the scent of pine.

"Is it well with thee, I ask every unsaved man and woman in this church today? Would you meet me in heaven if your Maker called us all home before the next opportunity to take your stand for Him?"

Brother Jim rolled up his sleeves. "Not enough *Amens!*" he bellowed. "If you could read the Lord's mind, just what do you suppose He would be thinking? Now, be reminded that He *can* read yours. He knows what evil lies in the hearts of men. Oh, you'll do better, you say? I'm telling you, my brothers and sisters, you *can't* do better—not by yourselves! It's been tried since the time of Moses. Those scattered tribes couldn't keep the law—and neither can you, not without God in your hearts! Satan's out after your soul and he's doing a good job with jelly-spined would-be do-gooders who keep trying to do it on their own. Give Him your heart . . . then get your hand on the plow and help Him out here below! He needs workers, field hands, *you.* Don't go telling me you love Him then be so heavenly minded you're of no earthly good! He's knocking . . . open the door . . . ask Him in."

Finished with castigating "both the sheep and the goats," Brother Jim took a dipper of water, gulped it down, and lowered his voice. "God loves you . . . wait not for the harvest . . . the fields are white already . . . oh, come home—I *beg* you—come home—"

As if by signal, the congregation began to sing softly and pleadingly:

> Come home, come home,
> Ye who are weary, come home,
> Ear-nest-ly, ten-der-ly, Je-sus is call-ing,
> Call-ing, O sin-ner, come home!

The sound of hobnail boots grinding into the scarred floor broke the sacred silence. Unshaven miners knelt before the pulpit. Farmers, in bib overalls, joined them. And the lines so clearly drawn between them washed away in shuddering tears of repentance.

"One more time," Brother Jim exhausted from his emotional sermon, mopped his brow and whispered, "I have a feeling that the Lord is speaking to someone out there—so won't you come during this last chorus—"

He stretched out his great hand. And it was Roberta who took it!

There was a little ripple in the congregation as the weary-looking men moved over self-consciously to make room for so great a lady. One of the men (indeed, wasn't he the driver of the wagon which had stopped the day of the hailstorm to tell of its widespread devastation?) spread a red bandana on the floor on which Roberta could kneel. She dropped to her knees.

"Well, the Lord be praised," Brother Jim said with such humility that anyone could see the Lord had surprised him this time. Then, regaining his vim, he shouted out victoriously, "Now, what do you think, Satan? You and your triple-layered infamy . . . you assassin of character . . . you sponsor of harlotry, gambling, and bootlegging! We outwitted you, didn't we!"

The crowd sang on. And others may have gone to the altar. Courtney never knew. And it was doubtful if the audience knew either. Their eyes were closed and they rocked gently back and forth in what Mandy called "sorrowful rejoicing." But Courtney knew when her brother joined Roberta. His arms about Roberta's shoulders, Efraim wept openly. She had never seen her big brother cry. Until this shining moment, perhaps tears would have diminished him in her sight. But now they enlarged him beyond all human proportions. It was as the Lord Himself revealed to her that this was what Efraim was waiting for.

CHAPTER 37
The Glad Tomorrow

Roberta and Efraim took their departure. There was a sort of glory shine about Roberta. And " 'twas as plain as the nose on your face that Efraim was restraining himself until they were alone so he could pop the question," Cousin Bella said. Courtney was saddened to see her friend leave, but they would be together again soon. Together as sisters. The sister neither had ever had. It could have made a beautiful ending for Roberta's life story—had it not been for Rambling Gate. In their only moment alone, Roberta whispered to Courtney that Robert VanKoten had written the great place was to be her wedding present if ever she married, her dowry. But . . .

Courtney understood. Some things must be righted. And, as for her own life, there were so many *more* to make right. Much had happened. But she was convinced that far more lay ahead. There was saying *good-bye* (forever this time) to Lance. There were the twins and their uncertain future. And there was a destiny of her own to fulfill. A sense of fatigue, foreign to her nature, swept her being just thinking ahead. Unfinished business must remain just that for the present. Clint had his hands full at the mines . . . Efraim had a dozen cases involving the entire valley to resolve . . . and she had the care of the twins as well as bringing peace to the hearts of others—a calling she felt God expected her to answer. So the sense of waiting persisted.

* * *

Courtney and Lance parted without tears. Standing so close together she could hear the ragged rhythm of his breathing, they lingered before the painting of "Another Spring." Lance and Donolar had chosen a sunny corner of the library opposite the ancestral lineup. A place where the sun could touch the golden leaves and a little breeze could set them trembling in the mind's eye. The painting said so much, so much—so much more than the painter realized. It answered the age-old question: *If a man die, shall he live again?* One day the Lord would speak to his heart in answer to her fervent prayers. And then the tree of life would burst into eternal bloom.

"A penny for your thoughts." Lance's voice trembled a little.

"They are worth much more. But they are not for sale."

"Dear, sweet Courtney, will you write to me?"

"Of course!" Courtney said stoutly, holding back the tears.

There was a whistle of a quail below. Donolar's signal that the buggy was hitched and ready. Lance turned from the painting, lifted Courtney's hand, planted a kiss in the palm, and closed it. Forever she would hold it like that—the tender memory of a childhood gone. . . .

* * *

Clint, sensing that she would be lonely, had promised to come home tonight. In fact, he would remain at the Mansion today if it were possible. She understood, did she not, that the farmers wanted to get the wheat seeded and that would leave the mines shorthanded? Yes, Courtney understood. But understanding did not take the loneliness away.

Much needed her attention, but a brisk walk would put life back into its proper perspective. Not far. Maybe just to the wheat field.

Bundled in a long wraparound coat, Courtney walked briskly a few minutes and then stopped. How clear. How bright. How beautiful. In the flurry of farewells this morning she had failed to note that the freezing weather had arrived on schedule. And, sure enough, the farmers were bent low, dropping the precious seeds with such concentration they appeared to be counting each grain. The frigid weather which was sure to follow would chain them in until nature brought them from the grave with new bodies—legions of green shoots that, in their new resurrection, held out no fear for their natural enemies.

The men were singing as they labored. Why not? If this crop matured, they could meet their payments at the bank. Already they were seeing another springtime, a glad tomorrow when they were back in the fields to stay. For now, the joy of planting had eclipsed the dark cloud of unpaid mortgages. Horace Bellevue might never show his face again.

* * *

The wind was blowing as forecast in the *Farmer's Almanac* when Clint, his body braced against its force, came into the clearing. The twins spotted him and darted past Courtney before she could restrain them.

Clint dismounted and, not bothering to tether his horse, scooped Jordan and Jonda to him, tucking them beneath his overcoat. They squealed with delight, but his face was sober. "Get some wraps, you two, if you want to ride with me to the stable!"

"Don' wan' toats—no!" Jordan began.

"Coats, you do. Without them, you do not. It's that simple."

170

Coats they did! Courtney thanked her husband with shining eyes. The depression had passed. She, too, faced the morrow gladly.

CHAPTER 38
Thanksgiving Announcement

Was autumn always so glorious? Courtney, slipping a woolen hood over her dark hair, decided that she had a lapse of memory every season—never remembering quite how glorious the bright woods, dusted with snow, could be in the great Northwest or how green and vocal in spring. The wheat was already resting in its winter bed and the rest of the world was yawning. As long as the world stood, the seasons would come and go. God's promise gave her reassurance that spring would give the earth an early wake-up call.

But there was something different in the air today—something that sent a tingle of excitement to her very fingertips, something that made her breathe shallowly. It was as if the time of waiting were about to end. And that made no sense at all. The only thing of significance was her acceptance of an invitation to accompany Doc George on his round to check on two families whose children had whooping cough. "Wear something warm and ready for the fire around Mandy's wash pot," the doctor had advised. "We will have to burn our garments and scrub with lye soap to make sure we don't bring the germs to the twins. Dangerous stuff, whooping cough—and those two can whoop it up enough without a disease!"

Why, then, the excitement?

Doc George's faithful old horse must have felt it, too. The ancient steed shook his head, snorted, and kicked up his heels. Steam shot from his graying nostrils. The buggy lurched forward and Courtney felt a little stitch in her side. It passed and she made no mention of the slight discomfort.

"You do think Cousin Bella's cold will clear up?" she asked instead.

"Easy boy, remember our age," Doc George said, tightening the reins. He chuckled then. "Of course, Arabella will be all right. Rest is the best medicine, although I did bully her into sipping a cup of pennyroyal tea to induce a good sweat." He chuckled again, "What a face she can make—had to threaten to boil a polecat and drench her with the juice to make her polish it off. Funny thing," he said, reining in slightly to negotiate a curve, "how the young worry about their elders while the elders worry about the young. Always was that way, I reckon—"

The pain came again. Courtney leaned forward and shifted positions.

"Come to think of it, you do look a little peaked—"

His voice was lost in the roar of Courtney's ears as the earth and sky changed places. Her body was as light as thistledown and would have floated away had her legs not weighed 300 pounds. What was that noise? Her stomach growling? Clutching it where the pain was worst, it felt shrunken, caved in like the cheeks of a drying apple. She felt herself slump forward in a welcome world of twilight where there was no sight, no sound, just the feel of motion as the buggy creaked and swayed . . . and the twilight gave way to darkness.

When Courtney decided to open her eyes so they could resume the journey, she found herself—to her total dismay—in her own bed! Doc George's face swam before her and then came into focus.

"I sent the others away, so we could talk," he said. "Why haven't you told me you were pregnant?"

"*Pregnant?* I'm not—" Courtney gasped and stopped. Even in her weakened condition, she recognized it was

ludicrous that the patient should deny a doctor's diagnosis.

"You disappoint me, child," Doc George said,
attempting to make his voice light. "Here you pray and
pray and then deny the answer!"

Courtney hardly heard. Of course. It all made sense
now. Her fatigue. The stress over little things. The discomfort of a corset—

"When?"

The doctor laughed outright. "I was about to ask *you*.
You young folks are never much help in nailing down
a date. But I would say you are entering your fourth
month—"

Courtney sat bolt upright. "You mean—you mean—
oh Doc George, how could I have missed the symptoms?"

"How could either of us? Give me all the details you
can. This could be a difficult case—mind you, I said
could be—"

"If you have any idea of terminating "

"Now whatever put *that* idea into your pretty head?"

Courtney told him then about her visit with Doctor
Ramsey and begged him not to upset Clint with the
potential danger of another miscarriage or a difficult delivery. "He would put me to bed the whole nine
months!"

"Six!" the doctor answered.

And it was only afterwards that she realized he had
made no promise.

*   *   *

Downstairs a few minutes later, Courtney was assur-
ing everybody that she felt fine—absolutely wonderful.
And it was true. Doc George broke the glad tidings to his
wife as he did not want Courtney exposed to her cold.
Mandy's joyful moanings, "Oh, my po' sweet baby"

brought Mrs. Rueben running from the chicken coop where she was fanning her calico skirts to drive a cocky bantam rooster in for his own protection. He and a big Rhode Island Red were at war, not to mention that the pheasants were finding no food in the fields and marching right up in an attempted *coup*. She would bake Courtney some of her special *Zwiebelkuchen*. Pshaw! jest plain ole onion bread, Mandy said darkly, when what her baby needed was chicken 'n dumplin's, so Miz Rueben could jest march herself right back to dat coop 'n wring de neck off'n dat feisty bantie.

"Now, now, *please*! Believe it or not, women have been having babies for years—" Courtney began.

"But not *this* baby!"

The three startled women turned to see Clint enter the front door walking on his hands, his feet, still in boots, flailing awkwardly in mid-air!

* * *

For the next two weeks the prospective parents walked with what Doc George called "an air of expectancy." Fingers laced. Arms linked. Eyes wide with wonder. "When?" Clint kept asking. "In the springtime—April, most likely," Courtney kept answering. They fell more and more deeply in love—more in love than Courtney realized she had the capacity to love. Rashly she promised Clint a son. But he *loved* girls, he protested. "True! But, my darling," she smiled from her corner of the cloud on which they sat, "we must remember the family name!"

Courtney wished that she could capture the stirrings in her heart the way Lance captured a scene on canvas. Autumn had withdrawn reluctantly and winter whistled through the canyons but kept his hoary beard hidden as if to torment the farmers. Leaves had lost their color; but the heavy snow was yet to come. November wore a somber cossack. And yet there was a mysterious stirring—a feeling that something wonderful was about to happen. The evergreens spoke of it as the sharp winds strummed their needles.

And then came the snow. A regular blizzard on Thanksgiving Eve. Early, valley folk said. And that was good. Just what the wheat needed. Courtney felt far removed from the wheat problem and basked herself before any one of the cheery fires crackling away in almost every room of the Mansion. Everything was going to turn out fine. Nothing could spoil Thanksgiving.

And nothing did. The next morning the sky had cleared and the sun burned on every tree and bush as if to set them ablaze. The crowds came early—some to clear the roads, some walking on barrel staves for snowshoes, others braving the drifts with their well-shod teams. True, some of the traditional trimmings were missing, but wasn't the wild turkey a bit less gamy this year? And everybody knew that acorn-fattened ducks made the sweetest meat. The Lord had provided well—and this was a "whole heap" better than their parents and grandparents had it, carving out civilization as they did under such harsh conditions. True pioneers, they were.

"We're all pioneers," Efraim said with an air of conviction. "No more mountains to climb or rivers to ford, but there are savages to conquer—those of ignorance and prejudice. There is still a jungle out there—"

"And praise the Lord, we still have the pioneer spirit with us today that God gave them yesterday—we welcome all Christian trailblazers," Brother Jim proclaimed just before the Thanksgiving prayer.

It was Jordan who said, "Our famb'ly's gonna have one, huh, Jonda?"

CHAPTER 39
For Better or for Worse

Courtney and Clint were to laugh many a time over the unexpected announcement. Between them, they had agreed to share the news with only the family circle in which they lived and postpone it indefinitely for the twins. Until Jordan and Jonda were better adjusted, felt more secure, so there would be no threat of the new arrival's stealing the love they had come to lean on. But Donolar, in his uncanny way, knew. The butterflies told him, he said. When Courtney laughingly told him that there were no butterflies now (quickly adding that they were sleeping in their silken cocoons), Donolar's great expressionless eyes looked upward. *His* butterflies were different, he said. They floated around in the sunshine above the clouds—probably helped paint rainbows—until spring.

And Donolar (or the butterflies) told the children. If Uncle Donny said it, it was so. It should be common knowledge. And valley folk could not have agreed more. Their excitement bordered on the ridiculous. "One would think we are about to give birth to a crown prince," Courtney remarked to Cousin Bella. Cousin Bella's eyes filled with unexpected tears which she wiped away in disgust. "He *will* be an heir to *our* throne," Arabella Kennedy Lovelace said with a lift of her chin.

Then and there Courtney decided *definitely* on a name. Why, even Cousin Bella knew it would be a boy!

* * *

176

December brought snow and more snow. "Angel feathers" the twins called it as they rolled and tumbled out-of-doors with Uncle Donny. That was a relief to Courtney because when they were around there were a million questions to answer. How did "Doc Santa" know when the baby was coming? What if God changed the date . . . and oh, Aunt Courtney, what if He made a mistake and sent the baby to the wrong house? Was she sure He had the right address?

But, all in all, it was a period of tranquility. Spirits were high among both farmers and miners. They had learned, Brother Jim said, not to put all their eggs in one basket. The Creator had plans for them all. There was buried treasure here—and who grubbed for the green and who for the silver didn't make a widder's mite of difference. Miners no longer looked upon their farming brothers as two-legged donkeys—and all that weeding, poking for grubs, and busting up clods—surprisingly—gave them backs equally as strong as those of the mining hands. And the farmers had decided that not all miners were harebrained dullards, too lazy to till the soil, and always on the lookout for some get-rich-quick scheme. Oh, there was the indebtedness. But loans were floated until June. By then crops would be reaped and marketed. Soooo, the preacher exhaled in relief, they had stopped behaving like the chart-class on the first day of school. . . .

Now, they could settle down and start thinking constructively. There was need of a school. *School!* Of course . . . and soon, Courtney realized. The valley was widening. Families were enlarging. It would be awhile before the baby needed formal schooling. But there were the twins—if—No *if's* about it!

The miracle of Christmas drew near. An ice storm turned the world into a giant wedding cake. Mandy and Mrs. Rueben began their baking and—in the true spirit of the season—co-mingled German recipes with soul food. Cousin Bella wondered if people could travel. Doc George said they could always skate.

Courtney, excitement coloring the pure oval of her face, looked more like a madonna than ever, Clint said repeatedly. Courtney caught his adoring eyes in her venetian mirror, and saw the resemblance he had first recognized. She saw, too, that even the soft folds of the maternity dress Cara had made for her failed to alter the unsophisticated another-world look that had so distressed her mother. Nothing, she supposed, would ever erase the essential simplicity of appearance which spoke of directness of the inner self.

"Oh, I am glad you like me the way I am!" she burst out on that one particular occasion when they were reexamining the layette Clint had given her before they lost the first child. "I—I guess every woman thinks she has lost her appeal when—when—"

"When she is about to give a man the world's most precious gift? Come here, you!"

"Clint," she whispered moments later, "what shall we do for the twins? I have been unable to shop—but it is Christmas—"

"I have been thinking of that. What about the Chinese imported toys we bought on our honeymoon—remember?"

Remember! "Perfect," she murmured—meaning his suggestion, the man who made it, and the beautiful winter-wonderland God had provided.

* * *

Maybe the guests *did* skate. Courtney, bubbling with happiness, would have failed to notice. She only recalled the twins, buttoned into their red suits and matching leggings . . . their model behavior and their delight with the hand-painted Oriental toys, the rag dolls Mandy had stuffed, the sleds Donolar made—and how they obediently shared with less fortunate children. In the midst of it all, Efraim and Roberta arrived, bringing in enough packages to overload a barge, dropping them beneath the giant evergreen, and began embracing everybody within reach in wild abandon. What had happened to the polished attorney who, unknowingly, maintained a courtroom manner in almost every situation? And the once self-consciously awkward girl who felt herself unlovely in the eyes of the man she loved?

Efraim did not keep her guessing. "Order in the court!" he called out above the tumult as, using an umbrella for a gavel, he pounded against the settle. "Miss VanKoten has consented to be my wife!"

Who in the world ever could have thought Roberta plain? Happiness made her radiant and Courtney told her so, pressing her lips to her future sister-in-law's ear to drown out the noise of a stampede of well-meaning friends who pressed forward to wish them well.

"When will you be married?" she asked the blushing Roberta.

"Soon—very soon, I think. Efraim does not want me to live alone—"

"You are welcome here. There are rooms galore on the third floor—"

"I know, but business is pressing Efraim that will keep him in the city—and we do not want to be apart. There is so much to plan—like where we will live—"

Courtney drew back. "Why, at Rambling Gate, of course! Can you think of a more wonderful arrangement than our being so near each other?"

Efraim, who was studying his bride-to-be's flushed face, must have seen it grow pale. He tried to elbow his way to the girls but was blocked by hearty whacks on the back, hand-pumping, and good-natured teasing about giving up his freedom for a ball and chain and a prison uniform.

The words rose above the tumult, causing Roberta's face to drain of the bit of color that remained. "I'm not sure I can live there, Courtney—not ever—after all that has happened—"

And may be happening yet, Courtney's heart finished for her. But Roberta was rushing on. "Efraim wants the place. He feels that a town is sure to spring up around the mines . . . businesses . . . schools . . . stores . . . and he wants to be a part of it with Clint. But me—well, I would settle for a little cabin high upon a mountain, just the two of us away from—danger. I'd like some old-fashioned rockers, a pie-crust table, ruffled curtains—nothing matching, no particular period. Just *us!*"

The look of anticipation was back. Roberta looked as if she had been racing downhill on a bobsled—intoxicated from skimming over the snow. Courtney knew the look. She knew the feeling, too. But one could not escape life. Vanessa had tried. . . .

Suddenly the crowd melted away. Clint had made his way to Courtney and now the four of them were standing together as if by prearrangement. And it was. Efraim turned to Clint, "As I was saying, it is time that our Courtney knew what her most important Christmas gift is to be!"

"My *what*? You are changing the subject too fast. I have had no time to wish Roberta the best God has to offer—or congratulate you—"

Efraim laughed deeply and richly—the laugh of a man in love. "You will have years for that. For better or worse, she's mine, *mine*, MINE!"

Clint reached out and drew Courtney to him. "He has forgotten his mission, darling. Your brother had intended telling us that 'for better or worse' the twins are to be ours."

CHAPTER 40
Waiting

Waiting. The feeling was back. Was life always going to be like this?

Courtney had hoped when Efraim told her and Clint that Jordan and Jonda were their children all matters were settled. Instead, there remained countless details—some of them frightening. Efraim locked Vanessa's letter surrendering the twins to the Desmonds in his safe after having it recorded at the county seat. There was nothing on record showing any claim by Horace Bellevue, although Efraim cautioned Courtney that Hiram Oakley could not be dismissed lightly. The man would sell his grandmother for a dollar; and, since he had served as Horace Bellevue's lawyer in making a grab for the wheat farmers' ground, he was not to be trusted. If he had another copy . . .

But Courtney was not to fret. Efraim and Roberta were in contact with ethical attorneys who were checking the validity of the Bellevue claim.

"Vanessa was irresponsible and eager to shed any parental responsibility, Courtney," Efraim explained. "But I have to believe that even she would have sensed greed in Clint's half brother. Nevertheless, we must protect the children, so I will leave no stone unturned."

"The idea of anyone else's taking them is unthinkable! What are you doing to insure their protection?"

"A great deal, darling. Please—you are not to upset yourself. Remember the baby—"

"You mean Jordan and Jonda's new brother?"

"Oh, so you have decided on the gender," her brother laughed.

Courtney sighed. "That was never a problem. I only want to make sure that the newest Desmond has an older pair of siblings—so share with me what you are doing. I know so little of these things."

Efraim held her hands and smiled reassuringly. "It is in our favor that there is no record of adoption, no falsified documents. I have 'WANTED' posters up in post offices throughout the Northwest. And, before the judge can declare you legal guardians—or parents, if you prefer—"

"I prefer!"

"It is essential that we post legal notices. Newspapers are best for this—*The Oregonian, The Statesman, Washington* . . . well, all of them, and would you believe in England as well? I doubt if the Grecho family, wanting no part in the whole sordid affair, will react except in embarrassment, but let's cover our bases all the way."

"Yes, let's."

If the newspapers could spare space for human need, they were improving, Courtney thought wryly. Usually, their printed matter devoted itself to politics, harking back to the Whigs and the Tories, disputes over long-ago-settled territorial rights, and taxation without representation.

It would be nice if all went smoothly. Nice but unlikely. But Efraim was right. She must leave legal matters in his hands—and the future in God's. She must *wait*. Wait for custody of the twins. Wait, along with Clint, for the spring wheat to relieve the financial burden. And wait while trillions of cells assembled themselves in her body to become a miracle encased in flesh.

CHAPTER 41
Love Letter

Temperatures plunged in January. Bitter, biting cold remained until the end of February. Never, old-timers said, had the ground been so solidly frozen. And never had the mountains been so completely covered with snow. Was the valley doomed to disappear altogether?

Travel became almost impossible. Miners complained. Some were convinced that Kennedy Mines should abandon their diggings until a thaw. A few stragglers drifted away. The more zealous, encouraged by Clint's promise of larger shares should they strike another rich vein, kept picking away. And, of course, wheat farmers were delighted.

Confined to camp, the men—inspired by Efraim's previous comments about a town at the site—constructed dreams in advance as they huddled together for warmth around a roaring campfire between shifts. There should be a commission house, a boardinghouse, and a bank with an oversized vault. Eastern companies were manufacturing fireproof ones now. And, sadly, there would have to be a jail. Should be brick with plate-iron bars on the windows. Maybe a hotel, a dry goods store, and Old Man Goettel was well-schooled in the art of cooperage. Could be he would like to go in with that young wagon maker and make barrels in case there was a gristmill. Three new sawmills were already in the building stage. Word had it that the owners were putting up some respectable-looking double-log houses. Jewelry? Well now, there was that fellow claiming he knew how to refine freshly mined silver into bracelets and belt buckles . . . and if prosperity came knocking, why not open the door and let a barbershop in?

The town would grow slowly, of course. Matter of fact, back in Old St. Joseph, folks used to put up false fronts, real spacious-like, and enterprising merchants swarmed in like honeybees attracted to clover. Leased 'em all before the boards were sawed and hammered down.

But the heart of the conversation, Clint was to tell Courtney later, was talk of the school and church. Mission schools had become "a mite worldly" way-back-when, even for Jason Lee, what with the "mixed breeds and all." And almost all the first schools were founded by the Protestant churches. Now public schools were coming into their own. Given a choice between a new house and a new set of books for the valley children, one man said, he would cast his vote for the books! Not necessary, another said wisely. Word had it that free schools were on their way—public and available to all, supported by the government . . . well, with *some* help from local taxpayers. The gap was closing between the coming of the first pioneers and the adoption of a workable system. And all agreed no price was too high for their offspring to be "learnt somethin'." Name? Well, there was "St. Helen's," sitting in the shadow of the mountain as they were.

It was Brother Jim who intervened. "That name ought to be reserved for the big, new church," he said. "Much as we love our little house of worship, its ribs are caving in. Besides, it's crowded as is and bring in all the newcomers—well, a new tabernacle is in order. The Lord's delivering us from our wanderings in the wilderness of poverty, so He deserves an altar built by the Mosaic blueprint! There are good women among us who can weave fine wool and linen. Others who can make

185

candles. And, if there's to be a silversmith, his first
obligation is the molding of silver candlesticks. I can see
it behind my eyeballs—the blue, the purple, and the
scarlet of it—made of fine pine, sweet balsam, and
acacia wood! Can you see it? 'Tis best I preach on Exodus
next meeting time! Do I hear an 'Amen'?"

The response was tumultuous.

All this when the wheat matured.

* * *

Blizzard followed blizzard. When finally Clint plowed
his way through the storm wearing snowshoes, he brought
three gifts to Courtney which he handed to her when at
last she unclasped her hands from around his neck and
he could breathe. One was a long-flowing, ruby-colored
robe with a mandarin neckline and wide pockets. "Oh, I
love it!" Courtney said with tears in her eyes. "And I love
you," Clint whispered huskily. "The color is nice and
warm—and the style leaves the baby room to grow." Her
arms were around him again when she felt something in
the pockets of the robe between them.

One held a small white Bible. The other held a letter
from Lance. The Bible was inscribed: "To Mommy and
Baby, from Dad." Courtney was so touched that she
forgot the letter altogether.

How much she loved this man God had given her. At
this moment, as they looked ahead as partners in bringing a baby into the world, Courtney may have loved Clint
partly because he reminded her of her father—that
gentle, sweet man with the sturdy backbone, faith in
God, in himself, in others, and in the righteousness of
his course. They could take misfortune in stride and
press toward the mark without expecting perfection.

All this she wanted to say. But a little breathless "I
love you" was all she could manage. Surely it was the

emotional moment that caused the sudden, white-hot stabbing in her side again. One moment she was journeying to the stars. The next she was being plummeted to the frozen earth, every bone in her body dissolving with the pain. Darkness drew a veil over her face as she clung to Clint. Then, thankfully, it faded to a dove-gray.

"Tired, darling?" Clint asked softly when she did not move.

"I guess I am," Courtney responded, her tongue feeling too large for her mouth. "I will rest before dinner—and read Lance's letter—"

Clint swooped her up, laid her gently on the bed, and pulled the soft robe over her head. "I will light a fire—"

The children, unannounced, burst through the door, showering them both with kisses before Clint could suggest a better time. Beautiful . . . angelic with chocolate on their pink faces . . . sweet . . . indefatigably cheerful . . . and . . .

"Well-mannered little people," Clint said in awe. "Oh, my sweet, how I regret that you have had to do it all yourself—"

I had help, my darling . . . your inspiration . . . God watching over us . . . and the whole family supporting me. Thoughts. Not words.

"Tell Mother good night, Jordan and Jonda. Let her and the baby rest—"

Mother . . . Did Clint realize he had said "Mother"?

The twins giggled. "Goo' night, Mudder," Jordan said obediently. His sister added, "An' wheat dreams!" *Wheat!* Even they knew.

When Courtney awoke, she felt wonderful. Surely, she had dreamed the strange symptoms. Adjusting the light, she opened Lance's letter. By now, he would have told Mother about Vanessa's death, the twins, and the new baby. If so, his letter made no mention.

My very dear Courtney:

You are often in my mind, because you are ever in my heart. Not all dreams come true, and I must let go of the one in which you and I would be Lord and Lady Stardust. Childhood was a long time ago. I confess a sense of remorse; but, my dear Courtney, I am less sad after seeing your happiness and have but one request. Will you name one of the 12 little disciples for me—that is, after you have exhausted the list there: Clinton Jr., Efraim Jr., Donolar, George Washington, Jimmy . . . oh my! Why do I persist in assuming they will all be boys when I am so fond of sweet little girls who grow up to be sweet and gentle women? . . .

But let us not be maudlin. Some dreams do come true—like this one for me. I guess, if I dared open the inner chambers of my heart, I would find that my true bride is my work. I am finding much to paint here. I do believe that Roberta's father would have me paint the whole of Europe for him. I will concentrate on France and England. But how can one ignore the other countries?

There is one place in particular that reminds me of our childhood fantasies. Over the neck of Scotland, narrowed by its twin firths, the air is crisper, the light is paler, and (as in Washington) for much of the year there is snow on the distant mountains. Here pipes play among the heather coming mysteriously from the spiced woodlands overlooking the moors. Ah yes, it catches the heart of the exile . . . but it is no more lovely than the great Pacific Northwest and not once have I seen a wood nymph as lovely as "Her Majesty" (now her husband's "madonna").

Your mother is happy at last, dear Courtney, surrounded as she is by her castle, an endless staff

of servants, friends of "high society," and an adoring husband. Perhaps I envy the VanKotens a bit.
They remind me of what you and I might have
shared in later years . . . and so it is, my darling,
that I shall write to you no more lest I covet my
neighbor's wife (you see, I HAVE learned a bit from
you!). I thank you for our beautiful sweet bird of
youth together . . . regretting only that I never once
received a love letter from you which I could tuck
close to my heart as I grow old and moustached in
my ivory tower—painting and pining away . . .

My love,
Lance

Postscript: Mr. VanKoten read with interest your
brother's legal notice regarding Vanessa's children.
And now, may I wish for you a thousand "Another
Springs." L.S.

Courtney folded the letter away, her mind whirling
with a myriad of emotions. Sadness for a childhood
gone. Affection for Lance who might never know that
there were a million kinds of love. Sorrow for her mother
who knew a love of *things* but not people. And pity for
the Grecho family who denied themselves the love of
two beautiful grandchildren. Slowly and deliberately,
she took from her desk a small Bible and inscribed it for
Lance: "A love letter from our Lord!"

CHAPTER 42
A Child Is Born

One day it was winter. The next it was spring. The Chinook winds blew in to rob winter of its tyrannical regime. Warm rains disrobed the lower mountain slopes of their ermine capes. Sheets of ice dissolved from field and stream and the migrating birds came home, filling the air with song. High-reaching mountain peaks held fast to their heavy snow pack, but below them the hills were scalloped with brown, bare earth. And farther down, in the valley, the new-green of wheat! Wheat that speared the ground with such force and determination one would think the shoots were assembling for all-out war against the forces of nature.

Fallow had turned to fertility. And the same wondrous transformation had taken place inside Courtney's body. As the sun and showers of April joined forces to unlock the miracle of growth, she, too, was ready to let go of her private miracle as had Mother Earth. The feel of waiting was over.

"There's a hospital I've looked in on," Doc George suggested. "Under the circumstances—"

Under what circumstances, Doc George—tell me! But, of course, she did not wish to know. Doctor Ramsey was wrong. She would deliver this baby with no problem—this beautiful, perfect baby who would fill the empty cradle in her heart. Had the discomfort meant anything, it would have happened long ago. It was natural for everyone to be overly concerned after her first loss.

"One does not miscarry in the ninth month," she said lightly. "Forget the hospital. Forget the nurses. And a fig for tradition! I want my husband with me every step of the way!"

"Clint?" Doc George's round, pink cheeks lost some of their color and he ran quick fingers through his cloud of white hair—his gesture of frustration. "Why, I'd have two patients at once. He would need the smelling salts with the first labor pain. This, young lady, is a woman's job—"

"Why, doctor!" Courtney said innocently. "Are *you* backing out?"

Doctor George Washington Lovelace lifted his hands in resignation.

* * *

"Right on schedule!" Doc George seemed pleased with his calculation of the date. "April 15, high noon, warm and sunny," he said when Courtney experienced the first contraction. "Now, to bed this minute! Arabella, please see that Donolar goes for Clint doing double-time. Send Mrs. Rueben with extra linens and make sure that Mandy keeps the fire going. Entertain the twins any way your creative minds can think of *except* letting them know what's going on. Otherwise, it will take all of you to corral them—"

Courtney bent forward with the pressure of the next contraction, her gown halfway over her head. "Eight minutes—" the doctor announced, turning his face away as she struggled with the garment.

"Breathe deeply—in, hold it, *out*! Think of the contractions as pressure—not pain—"

Courtney exhaled and giggled. "Some day," she said, "there will be *lady* doctors. You wait and see. Then you men can learn from them what childbirth is all about."

Another pain—no, *pressure*. Courtney breathed deeply, exhaled, and lay back exhausted. Again . . . and again . . . was it getting dark or had someone drawn the drapes? Mrs. Rueben *had* been there, had she not?

"You're doing fine. Here—bite on this."

Doc George slipped what felt like a piece of leather between her clenched teeth. She spat it out. "I don't need a bridle bit! I—I need—I need Clint!"

"Here, darling, *here!*" And, praise the Lord, Clint was entering the door, a mask of gauze over his pale face. "How long has this been going on, Doc?"

Courtney heard the word *hours*, felt Clint take her hand, and then the world stopped turning. Gravity lost its pull and she floated off into a dark space where there was no pain—no, *pressure*. . . .

Clint was bathing her forehead when she made a brief return from the world of darkness. "Breathe deeply, darling," he pleaded with tears in his voice. "Inhale—"

The cry Courtney heard was her own. The pressure was back—and translated however Doc George wished, it was *pain*. Hard, racking pain that twisted her body grotesquely. Then another . . . another . . . and another. . . .

She was floating again, her heavy body now lighter than air, only to be dropped into an ocean of sweat and tears. *Tread*. That was what she must do, Courtney thought, remembering the awful nightmare of trying to hold her baby's head above water . . . save it from drowning.

"Things aren't going well!" The doctor's voice or her husband's?

"Clint!" she screamed when the worst pain of all invaded her weakening body.

"Right here, sweetheart—oh, my darling, I am so proud of you—"

The voices blurred then. Words floated around in the bedroom, bouncing against the beams and dropping to the carpet . . . *heartbeat . . . umbilical cord . . . twisted . . . happens in nature . . . fetus . . .*

No! Courtney's heart revolted. *Not fetus. Baby!* Skip statistics. Love was stronger than death . . . many waters could not quench it . . . floods could not drown it. She had God's word! This baby would live.

With supreme effort, she moved back into the world of dimension, bringing into focus Clint's face, pale as death. She tried to smile, failed, and gripped his hand with all her strength. Doc George tore him from her. "Give me a hand—*now!*"

Courtney prayed. She would never remember the words. Neither would she convince others that God's answer was in the form of shining white creatures hovering over her with healing in their wings. Wings? Yes, she heard the soft whirring. And her last conscious thought was *Angels really do have wings . . . I can hardly wait to tell Brother Jim . . .*

"I have never seen a mother try so hard or a father *cry* so hard!" Doc George's jovial voice came from a far-distant land. "Here is your reward."

He placed a tiny bundle, wrapped in a blue flannel receiving blanket, in Clint's arms. Dumbfounded, his eyes drooping heavily in an ashen face, the new father accepted his son. Yes, *son!* The blue blanket announced to a waiting world that Kennedy Clinton Desmond had joined the human race.

Humbly, Clint laid the baby beside her. Together, they opened the blanket to see a pair of blue, blue eyes staring up at them inquisitively below a fuzzy tuft of gold curled in a question mark. "Oh yes, precious one, you are ours. The angels brought you straight from heaven," Courtney whispered.

The twins had broken rank and were storming the door. They bounced on the bed and stared in wonder.

"Anudder *us*," Jordan whispered in awe. "Huh, Jonda?"
Jonda's reply was lost in Cousin Bella's shout of triumph,
"Another Kennedy!" An exhausted doctor shook his white
head. "Another *miracle*," he said.

CHAPTER 43
Eruption!

Courtney experienced no postpartum depression. Instead, she drifted through her days in a state of euphoria. The baby was perfect. His father was perfect. Life was perfect. Forgotten were the wheat, the mines, the loans, the status of the twins. Nature graciously erased the disappearance of Horace Bellevue and Lum Birdsey as well as the cold, calculating, darting eyes of Hiram Oakley, so that the new mother could accustom herself to the almost unbearable joy of helping God create.

"Ten fingers, ten toes, eyes like yours—oh Clint!"

It was Clint's last day home. There was a problem that needed resolving at the mines, he told Courtney. Somebody had smuggled liquor into camp. There he stopped. Courtney, twisting the buttercup curl on top of their baby's head, had not heard. Nor should she. Not until she was stronger.

Mother and child. "Oh darling, I could never have stood it if anything had happened to either of you. I love you both more because you are a part of each other—and a part of me that I could never have let go—"

"Let go? Why, it was a breeze—nothing to it—"

Clint groaned. "I was *there*, remember? And you never fooled me for a minute—you told me over and over about your fears—the danger—"

Courtney jerked herself erect in the cricket rocking chair. "Clint Desmond! I did no such thing. I protected you—"

Clint groaned again. "*Protected* me! Worrying is what husbands are for—worrying and loving their wives and children. Through them, God gives men an earlier heaven!"

"Oh Clint—my darling, my darling—did ever a couple share such a love as the two of us?"

"I doubt it."

Why bother to tell her she talked in her sleep?

* * *

People came and went. Admittedly, the Mansion-in-the-Wild was a child-centered home for the first three weeks of young Kennedy's life. Arabella walked with even greater dignity. Mandy and Mrs. Rueben resumed their feuding over who was to bathe little Kennedy until Cousin Bella intervened and said the two of them were to stagger the days. One harsh word from either and all rights would revert to the innocent party! Doc George weighed the baby daily on the spring scale used for measuring medications and reported each gram of increase. Brother Jim, holding him awkwardly but remembering to support the tiny head, called him "David, a baby after God's own heart." Did Courtney know that David meant *beloved*? And didn't she know that this child was a "chosen one," one who would slay many a Goliath in his lifetime? It was Donolar who introduced him to poetry—all the nursery rhymes and rhyming prayers. It was Donolar, too, who explained that God sent Baby Ken on the wings of butterflies. After all, He created *all* creatures. And it was Donolar most likely who saw to it that Jordan and Jonda felt no jealousy, just pride and a great love for the baby God had molded in their image.

Efraim and Roberta came when the "miracle child" was three weeks old. They had been unable to come sooner because of something far removed from Courtney's mind—"the pressure of business." They would combine their visit with a trip to Rambling Gate. It had been neglected far too long.

And that is how, by strange coincidence, they came to be at the ancient inn when the terrible disaster struck. The disaster such as settlers of the frontier had never heard tell. The disaster which would change all their lives forever . . . from generation unto generation.

*　*　*

"He's beautiful," Roberta breathed, her eyes dream-filled.

"Of course," Courtney said smugly. "And baby makes five instead of three," she added as Roberta handed Kennedy to Efraim and pulled up a chair beside Courtney. "At least, I hope the adoption—"

Efraim maddeningly ignored the question in her voice. "This lad looks enough like me to be my own."

He blushed scarlet and Roberta followed suit. *Ah, young love!* But thank goodness, their embarrassment brought Efraim back to the adoption. There appeared to be no contest. One of his several legal matters in progress was to represent the Desmonds before Judge Brumstein, see that the procedure was duly recorded (yes, he had the papers for their signature!), and have the petition locked in the vault.

They talked at length, carefully avoiding mention of Horace Bellevue's threat—undoubtedly as empty as his head—although a million questions filled Courtney's mind. It was Roberta who swung the subject away from the matter. Standing to smooth an imagined wrinkle from her amber suit which made her complexion look like ripe peaches, she said with chagrin, "Forgive me, Courtney, how are *you* feeling?"

"Physically, 'in the pink,' as Doc George would say. Emotionally—well, I am *up* when I look at your nephew and *down* when Clint is away. And nephew reminds me, have you two set the date?"

"Easter Sunday!" Efraim's voice was as victorious as if he had won his most difficult case.

Donolar's roses would be in full bloom, Courtney cal-culated quickly. And, of course, she and Clint would stand up with them. He would be less busy then—except for some problem he had mentioned. Did Efraim know of it?

Efraim did.

He inhaled deeply, frowning as if the air held no oxygen. "That old demon rum. Clint spends more time underground than a mole so was unable to track down the source. We still haven't. But at least I witnessed a delivery. Would you believe it was stashed away beneath a load of manure? The shrunken body of the driver of the wagon belonged to a man as old as Methuselah— skin cross-grained and a snarl of gray hair that hung to his belt. Talk about stench! It was a toss-up among body odors, stale liquor, and the load he was hauling from the cow pen! He was drunker than one of Brother Jim's so-called hoot owls—with a jug beside him—kept pulling out the corncob and having a snort—" Efraim paused, all but gagging with the memory.

Roberta's face was chalky. "Where did it come from?"

"I wish I knew! I only know where it went. Some of the newer hands bunched around him handing over what must have represented a month's pay for jugs he had covered with fertilizer. Please never let Donolar know that the foul-odored stuff attracted a swarm of greedy little white butterflies—"

"Affirmative," Courtney nodded, striving for a light touch and failing. "How did you stop him? Did you corner the man—stop his bootlegging?"

"Unfortunately, none of those. He spotted me walking toward the wagon, gave the team a swat, and was gone. I would never have guessed such scrawny mules could run that fast. They had memorized their getaway plan—plunged across the creek and into the brush, leaving no tracks, not even an echo!"

A wave of nausea swept over Courtney. Foul as the odors the man and his load exuded, the contents of the jugs were more wretched. Undistilled, raw, and tasting like sheep-dip (Brother Jim described it), the stuff would eat a man's insides up and destroy his brain. Something must be done—*now*!

It seemed perfectly in keeping that there should be a low grumble of thunder—far away but earthshaking. At least, it would be good for the wheat if it rained but she hoped it would hold off until Clint could get home.

* * *

Efraim and Roberta had ridden away for what seemed only moments when the storm struck. Not the gentle April shower she had hoped for but a hard, driving rain. Not refreshing either. It was more like the monsoons of India. Hot. Steamy. Breathless even though there was a hard-blowing Chinook wind. Downstairs the shutters were banging. Mrs. Rueben and Mandy would attend to them. She, herself, must make sure the twins were with them or at Innisfree with Donolar. Hurriedly, she moved to close the windows which were contrary. In the few minutes it took to force them down she was soaked to the skin.

When the last one yielded, she remembered that she had forgotten the shutters. And in the moment she hesitated, weighing the wisdom of reopening the windows, Courtney saw the slight figure of a boy. The Laughtens' oldest? Barely distinguishable, he was looking over his shoulder in horror just as an explosion ripped the world apart followed by a flash of light. Even as she rushed to meet the boy, Courtney knew it could not have been electricity. The sequence was wrong.

CHAPTER 44
The Tender Grapes

Tearfully, Silas Laughten tried to explain. His mother had sent him to the Company Store. Mr. Bronson detained him " 'cuz uv th' storm." And then the "awfulest thang ever" happened—av . . . anvil . . . yes, *anvilanche*!

"Avalanche!" Courtney whispered in horror.

"*Grundlawinen!*" Mrs. Rueben shrieked from the downstairs linen closet.

"Yessum—rain loosened th' snow—'n besides, it's a-meltin' and th' river's a-fillin'—'n I gotta get my ma 'n th' kids 'cuz—it ain't safe hereabouts—'n th' bossman said—*I gotta get Ma!*"

Panting with fear, the half-drowned boy made a move to dash from the front porch. Hardly aware of her actions, Courtney grabbed at his sodden shirt. "Wait, Silas! The bossman—Mr. Clint—What did he say?"

The boy tore himself away. "We all gotta go t' Ramblin' Gate—"

Farther from the river was all Courtney could think— and Efraim was there. Dazed, she stared at the pool of water left where Silas Laughten had stood. Then, she reacted to the news. Life here on the frontier was filled with incongruencies. One must expect the unexpected. Maybe some part of her brain was recording all this. One day she would enter it in her journal . . . write that book . . . had Cousin Bella remembered to enter little Kennedy's birth?

Somehow they managed. Mrs. Rueben's scream had been the only hint of panic. Donolar appeared from nowhere, holding a twin—both hooded in raincoats—by either hand. As usual, they were in perpetual motion, dancing on one foot and then the other. But they showed no signs of fear, just excitement. Mandy bundled the baby in a patchwork quilt and grabbed an umbrella.

Details of the rapid exodus were never clear in Courtney's memory. Cara came, bringing along her brood—all silent with fear. Others joined them as Courtney hurriedly stuffed the baby's needs in a bag and shrugged into a coat. The one picture that lingered in her mind was the face of the mistress of Mansion-in-the-Wild. It was a mask with only the eyes burningly alive as she closed the great house for what possibly was the last time. And her control was more heart-wrenching than a burst of grief would have been. Dear Cousin Bella from whom Courtney had learned the definition of true courage.

They rushed into a dismal twilight. The rain had stopped. But the wind continued. Dancing. Twisting. Sweeping. Creating waves of light and shadow among the ferns and bringing the choking odor of a partially extinguished fire. Fire? When the enemy was snow? The women—with no time to think on the safety of their husbands—did not question, so intent were they to get their children to safety.

Cry tomorrow, Courtney thought when feeling began its slow return to her heart. But that did not preclude one backward glance. And what she saw caused her heart to stop momentarily and then explode. A tremendous cauliflower-shaped cloud hung motionless above the mountains in the chain behind them, just—*Oh, dear God, no!*—beyond the mines. St. Helen's? Its volcano was thought to be extinct. The source made no difference. That some powerful force had boosted the deadly gas skyward was enough. Even as she watched in horror, the unusual cloud lazily glided down the mountainside and stealthily crept toward the river. Just a small eruption could have done it, Courtney remembered from her geography. And the escaping gas, being heavier than air, would cling to the nearby hillsides, destroying the lives of those in its wake. Already the silence was oppressive, the animals restless—

Oh Clint, Clint, CLINT! But the sound she made was a warning scream, "Run! *Run* faster—RUN!"

Darkness fell. Pitch-black. Starless. Panic gripped at Courtney's throat. Were they the only human beings left on the planet? Certainly, the earth seemed to have been loosed from its gravitational pull and cast into the black pit of space. The rain had left a sticky dampness that was less refreshing than clammy, like the dead air escaping a tomb.

Courtney prayed fervently that nobody else would look back lest there be another fiery belch from the mountain's chimney. Nobody did.

And that undoubtedly accounted for the fact that what happened next was more disturbing to the others than to herself. To her, it was anticlimactic—near-comical—by comparison to what she had witnessed and what she feared. By now, had the deadly gases settled along the river like an early-morning fog? Were the men—no, *no!* She would not say *dead!*

It all happened so suddenly. One minute the evacuees were slipping, sliding, and falling down along the trail, feeling the brambles tear at clothing and flesh. The next, they were safe at Rambling Gate.

Safe? There was a beam of blinding light. A sound like an oncoming tidal wave. And the air was filled with screams. The ashen smell of smoke gave way to a pungent scent—familiar but unidentifiable to Courtney's nostrils. Fruit. That was it. The smell of rotting fruit. Grapes, once tender, now fermenting.

CHAPTER 45
Charge!

A few stars ventured through the clouds, coming closer and closer, then sneaking underfoot. Then the very heavens vanished, leaving nothing but noise. A world of noise. Courtney fought off the illusion. She must get her bearings. Holding the baby close to her breast, she crept closer to the bridge, her eyes trying to penetrate the darkness, focus on the light. And then it was on her, a lantern lifted high to illuminate dimly the outlines of figures squatted behind bushes for protection . . . Donolar and the twins . . . Cara's family . . .

And who on earth was shouldering her way through the undergrowth, crossing the bridge? It was not—it could not be. It was Arabella Lovelace.

For an incredulous moment Courtney stared at the erect, somewhat haughty, black-clad woman striding across the narrow bridge, completely deaf to Efraim's commands, "Go back! Go back this minute. There's a crisis here—"

"Precisely! And I have come to help. Ingrates—you mixed-up, misguided idiots! I know what you are up to. It all comes together now."

Again Efraim's voice. This time pleading. "Go back, I beg you—you've no idea what you are getting into. Hold still, Lum, before I have to cuff you! Go home, Cousin Bella—the troops are coming—and—"

"Home? We *have* no home. And maybe we have no family—partly due to these turncoats! If they had remained on duty—*bring me your umbrella, Mandy!*"

" 'Charge of the Light Brigade'!" Donolar cheered. He was unafraid? And the delighted laughter of Jordan and Jonda said that they, too, failed to recognize the danger.

Did they, in childish wisdom, understand the situation better than she herself understood? Courtney wondered. Cousin Bella must understand who the enemies were. Why wait for troops? The brave woman, through whose veins flowed the red blood of pioneer courage, could face death without flinching. Well, Arabella Kennedy Lovelace deserved some backup—armed as she was with only an umbrella!

Courtney leaned down to place the baby in Cara Laughten's arms. "And Mandy," she whispered, once she had picked out the ample squatting figure, "keep an eye on Donolar and the twins—and stay put, *all* of you. I have played this scene before."

Remembering the dramatic moment when the train bringing her West was robbed, she pulled the long, pointed hat pin from the sodden felt hat under which she had pushed her long hair. It was better than nothing. Then she, too, became a part of the "six hundred."

"Move over here, Roberta—bring that yard rake with you to hold this little weasel down!" Efraim's voice. So he was the one holding the lantern! But was that plow share his only weapon? Roberta took over with Lum Birdsey.

Efraim dashed forward and made an attempt to pull his cousin down.

From somewhere in the darkness behind the great house came a hoot of derision. "That's it, Yore Holiness! Hide behin' th' skirts uv that he-woman!"

"He-woman, is it now?" Cousin Bella's voice amplified into a scream of fury. "Think I don' know that blustering voice and its venom, Josiah Bunker? Promising the Lord like you did to abstain from partaking of spirits? And all the time sneaking around to still whiskey right under our very noses. Of all the ways for a hen-husband to piddlediddle his life away—"

"You're obstructing justice, Cousin Bella," Efraim was pleading in a voice that said he would resort to any wile to protect her. *"Cousin Bella—"*

He made a futile grab, but she shook loose and charged as if she were indeed leading those gallant men into the teeth of shot and shell in the Crimean War. All because someone had blundered. Someone had blundered again. This time it was Cousin Bella. In her rush to get at her victim, she failed to take into account that the woods were alive with his allies. They swarmed from everywhere. But Courtney saw only one. Horace Bellevue was standing just outside the pool of light made by Efraim's lantern and there was a suspicious bulge in the right-hand pocket of his plaid shirt. His chalky face stood out like a disembodied spirit with the rest of his silhouette lost in darkness. His restless eyes roamed the few faces confronting him. Then he withdrew the shiny object and aimed it at Efraim's back.

With a warning scream to her brother, Courtney sprang out of the shadows and with all her might jabbed the hat pin into the weapon-bearing arm. Caught off guard, Clint's half brother let out a roar of rage and dropped the gun. Efraim's foot was on it in a split second. And there was a moment when Courtney thought there was hope. Then the swarm of men descended upon them . . . surrounding them . . . and they were doomed as were the men in Tennyson's poem. In the volley of thunder that followed, Courtney was aware only that, God willing, the children were safe. Then the world of smell was added to the world of noise. Fermenting fruit. And the scent of ashes was back. . . .

CHAPTER 46
"Take Me to Your Leader!"

Wisely, Efraim extinguished the light. In the bedlam that followed, Horace Bellevue, still howling like a wounded animal, slunk into the bushes. How like him to desert his men. For there was little doubt that he had masterminded the illegal brewing of liquor in the tanglewood behind Rambling Gate. Why had nobody suspected . . . investigated the hissing . . . the strange odors . . . and his source of almost limitless funds?

Efraim had squatted, pulling Courtney and Roberta down beside him. "Stay down. I have the gun which I will use only if I must. Help is coming—"

"But who? How?" Courtney whispered back, thankful that her sanity was restored.

"Sh-h-h—Brother Jim was here, helping plan a garden wedding—we found the still. They were trying to destroy the evidence—set fire—"

"Then that was the explosion? Then what—?"

The whisper died on her lips. A powerful hand had clamped over her mouth. And a groan told her that others were struggling with Efraim and Roberta.

Lord, send help. It matters not how—just send it!

There was a blast of a bugle. Close at hand! And the measured cadence of what sounded like a thousand-man cavalry racing to the rescue.

"The troops!" The hand over Courtney's mouth dropped and a rush of footsteps said that the mob was attempting a wild getaway.

Too late!

The late-rising moon, which would put the lantern to shame, illuminated the scene of countless horses surrounding the area. The bugler? Why, it was none other than Brother Jim. And behind him was Doc George, fit as a fiddle.

"Not one false move!" the doctor ordered, extending his black bag. "I use this for more than delivering babies, contrary to popular belief. Right now, the bag is filled with nitroglycerine for my wife's heart. Even a sneeze can cause it to explode! Drop those weapons—now!"

Courtney's heart soared with joy at her answered prayer. Doc George's presence said that Clint and the other men at the mines must be safe. Else, would he have left? And the fact that he and Brother Jim were alive said that the poisonous gases had failed in their deadly mission.

But where were the troops? Guns were dropping to the ground, but . . .

And then she knew. These wonderful, wonderful people had added their usual touch of comedy. *They* were the troopers! Oh, officials would be along. But organizing took time. Time they did not have. And, meantime, they had saved a perilous situation. Averted a tragedy. And who could "hog-tie" the evildoer more efficiently than the settlers themselves?

Now came the battalion of infantry. Line after line. And last in line was Clint! She was in his arms being crushed to death and not caring. Clint, dear, wonderful Clint—the most wonderful husband and father in the world—was alive. Holding her. Kissing her. Murmuring terms of endearment.

"We're all fine," he whispered. "Nobody hurt—mines buried in snow, but we can dig out!" *But the volcano, Clint?* "Steam release due to pressure." *But the poisonous gases?* "It was as if the Chinook wind parted the atmosphere as the east wind divided the Red Sea to let the children of Israel pass. The vapors struck an updraft and were swept into the pass to dissipate—the horses are proof-positive. Animals would have been the first to perish. Someday old St. Helen's will blow—but for now—"

Yes, for now. For now, Roberta had surrendered Lum Birdsey to Brother Jim and lighted twin eight-lamp bronze chandeliers. Their sparkle was caught and held in the jeweled prisms circling their center rods to spill gold reflections dancing over the shadowy stairs. While the rest of the furniture looked like hunched-over ghosts in its protective wrapping, she had cleared the gate-legged cherry-wood table and converted it into a serving table. Women, their men and children safe, milled everywhere. Brewing coffee. Setting out cups. And singing softly, "Praise God from whom all blessings flow. . . ."

Courtney and Cousin Bella were not among them. There were still unanswered questions. There were investigations to make. And there were decisions to reach. A show neither of them chose to miss . . . and if a woman's opinion were called for . . .

The disarmed men, looking like whipped puppies, huddled in a knot as Clint wordlessly reeled out rope for John Laughten and Josh Thorson to tie their hands behind their backs then string them together like a catch of fish. Marshal Lindbloom and deputies Denver Carouthers and Sampson Smith would be along to deal with them properly. They fostered law and order. Until then, it would behoove every one of them to maintain a respectful silence. Anything they said could and would be used against them in a court of law!

Doc George, busily bandaging a few minor wounds, was laughing heartily. "Some woman, my wife," he said almost to himself as he bit off a piece of string and threaded a needle. "Imagine old Josiah Bunker's being intimidated by a he-woman wielding an umbrella!"

Josiah did not hear. He was cringing before Brother Jim. "I'm sick to the gills with the both of you!" The preacher, a long-simmering pot, had reached a boiling point. He shook Josiah with one hand and yanked at the collar of Lum Birdsey with the other. "It's a wonder the Lord don't up and spit in your faces! I'm guessing that He don't credit either of you two earwigs with brains enough to have thought up this particular brand of wickedness. So, if you value life here or hereafter, take me to your leader! *Where is Horace Bellevue?*"

Josiah cringed even more, near-rolling himself into a ball of fuzz. "I don' know nothin', Reverend Brother Sir—was I to know, I'd tell yuh—be merciful to me, a sinner—I don' know nothin' a-tall!"

"Right on both counts. Sinner you are, and a brainless one. All right, Lum. Where's Bellevue!"

Lum Birdsey's bloodshot eyes rolled like ball bearings. "It ain't him, Brother Jim—he—he dun' th' moonshinin'—'n paid me a mite t'hep out—but—but he had a boss, too. An' I don' know who—somebody real legal-like—that's all I know."

"Oh no, it's not! Spit it out, my boy. Get it off your chest. It's your last chance." He shook the little man until his teeth rattled from the motion. Courtney, watching, held her breath.

"Wait, wait . . ." Lum put up a claw-like hand in pleading. "I guess I be knowin' uh little—but I don' know *who*. You gotta protect me iffen I tell. They threatened t'kill me—*promise*—"

He would promise nothing until he heard the story, Brother Jim said. And Lum Birdsey had to be satisfied. His story was too dreadful to be fiction. Life was a struggle here. Surely Brother Jim could understand? Gone was them good old days when wild turkeys was a-gobbling everywhere and a man what wasn't a-mind to raise hawgs could buy a shoat for a dollar. Then, what with the

210

wheat a-failing . . . well, a man had to make a living,
didn't he just? Well now, in a way, maybe nature meant
the fruit and wheat hereabouts to be used up. Law, he
didn't know about, but them faraway lawmakers . . .
well, what did they know about frontier life? Yep, could
be natural-like (Lum's voice was rising with conviction).
All them apples and grapes. And all them foldin' hills
fer tuckin' away the stills. If 'tweren't legal, it oughta
be—

"Stop the rationalizing, Lum. Tell the story!"

Lum's bravado crumbled. Yessir. *Yessir-ee!* That devilish man at the top had oughta be exposed all right.
That's where the big profit went. Yeah, he fattened Horace Bellevue's bank account, but mostly it went to the Big
Man. He had Horace bring out sugar and nature fur-
nished the rest. Good, pure stuff, 'twas, he said with
some pride. But the Big Man could'n be satisfied like
common folks—got greedy, he did. Jest up 'n watered
the pure fruit uv th' vine down with water—plain ole
water. Had t'add wild onion roots an' red-hot pepper
t'give it bite. An' ("Oh parson, me—I'd never do such a
thang!"), th' profiteer topped it off with soap-makin' lye
t'give it a head o'foam—coupla men died from th' likes
uv it—

Lum Birdsey's confession was never finished. There
was a thunder of hoofbeats. A burst of fire, aimed at the
moon, exploded in warning. The officers had arrived.

But nobody was prepared for the prisoner who, hand-
cuffed, rode by their side. The marshal, rotund and commanding, barked orders. Two wiry men, bewhiskered
and wearing large sombreros, reined in beside the man
in handcuffs, their star-shaped badges flashing in the
moonlight.

"Howdy, folks," Marshal Lindbloom said in greeting
(and there was no mistaking the pride in his voice).
"Meet the leader of this gang!"

CHAPTER 47
Legend, Prophecy—
and Eternal Truth!

Hiram Oakley!

It was Efraim who, quiet until this point, sauntered casually to the four riders. All but Hiram dismounted.

"Thank you, marshal," Efraim said, extending his hand. "Did you find the situation as I described it?"

"A search warrant led to the evidence," Marshal Lindbloom replied. "And we're obliged to citizens like you. It was your being on constant surveillance from your office and the cooperation of Miss VanKoten here that pinpointed the long string of scams."

Courtney shook her head when someone offered her coffee. She must concentrate on every word. That her brother had been assisting was stimulation enough— and *Roberta*? Maybe some day she would understand— *if she listened*!

"We found Oakley on his way to make a delivery," one of the deputies offered. A statement which sent the lawyer into a tirade of words.

"False arrest!" His voice had risen so high that the words cracked like those of some overgrown boy's in delayed adolescence. "I'll sue for slander. You'll pay— I'll—" Hiram thought better of threats and, shifty eyes cast downward, he switched tactics. "You've got no real charges!"

"No charges?" Efraim's voice was dangerously low. "Try kidnapping . . . conspiracy to defraud the government . . . illegal transportation of goods. Try tax evasion . . . blackmail . . . and *murder*! At least two men have died from your poison. Where's Bellevue?"

"How should I know? Probably went to collect his children—"

Jordan and Jonda! Courtney cast a quick look over her shoulder. And, *praise the Lord*, there they were, one on each of Donolar's knees—the three of them watching raptly as if they were looking at a picture book.

But their custody? The next few moments would tell.

The marshal pulled an official-looking envelope from his breast pocket. "Here is what you asked me to confiscate as Exhibit A."

Hiram Oakley's attempt at a cry of triumph was more of a last gasp. "The papers their mother signed—"

Efraim's fists doubled. And then he exhaled and inhaled deeply. Why bother? "You miserable excuse for a man! Don't you think I know my sister's handwriting? Add forgery to the counts, marshal!"

Marshal Lindbloom's laugh came from below his belt. "The state of Illinois would agree with you. This man is an artist at forgery. When we're finished with him here, it'll be a toss-up between seven other states where he's wanted under a multitude of aliases!"

Courtney heard no more. The twins belonged to her and Clint by divine election, just as surely as did Baby Ken. Did she whisper her husband's name? *Something*— no, *Someone*—brought him to her side. She was in his embrace. But only for a breathless moment.

"Muv-ver," the wee-small voice of Jonda came from a screen of ferns. "Muv-*ver*!" Jordan's echo was louder than life.

Mother. What a beautiful word!

* * *

"Bustin' up stillin' " made quite a story. Two newspapermen visited Rambling Gate, but not a trace remained.

Copper kettle and coils were gone as were the sacks of sugar the law officers' noses had led them to. 'Twas the smell of smoke and sour mash that betrayed the still hidden in the brush. The barrels were there—empty. There was a mighty strange odor thereabouts and folks guessed the contents were dumped into the creek. Come to think of it, Old Man Ike Somers claimed his own cows acted mighty strange. Had their fill of "crick water" and commenced to "beller like bullfrogs," hiking up their tails and trying to jump over the moon. Milk might have been contaminated. Not that he'd drink it, mind you . . .

Horace Bellevue was never seen again—at least, not in the Columbia River Country. There were those who said so convincing were the Brothers that Bellevue, Washington, really *was* named for the family. This the settlers disputed as it made them look "suckered in." 'Twas a heap more likely, they told their children and grandchildren at story-telling time, that Horace Bellevue met with a fate similar to that of Ichabod Crane. True, nobody found a shattered pumpkin (head of the ill-fated Hessian who carried it on his shoulders!). But that was understandable. 'Twas the wrong season for "pun'kins." What they *did* find was a riderless horse, minus its bridle, quietly cropping grass near Horace Bellevue's hangout. And yep, sure as shootin', there were claims that somebody talked to somebody else who said his cousin heard a friend say he sighted the man in New York. . . . Yes, the woman in red who held onto his arm *could* have been Alexis Worthington Villard Bellevue. Mighty convenient, her having the same name since she was his sister-in-law. Two things were certain. The man's spirit never came back to reclaim his head. And that wicked witch of a woman gave up hope of leading that noble man, Clint Desmond, astray.

As for St. Helen's Mountain, if—perchance—it was the culprit that eventful night, it went right back into extinction. Of course, there were those who said the emission of steam was warning of another Sodom and Gomorrah. How many signs did folks need of the wrath to come against transgressors? People of that persuasion moved families and earthly goods elsewhere. But for every wagon that rumbled out, a dozen rumbled in. And their faithfulness was a "sweet savour" to the Lord. He rained down prosperity. . . .

* * *

Now, the story of Josiah and Lum was a lot different. In it was living proof that mankind, no matter how corrupt, could be reconciled when he repented of his sinful ways. Might have gone on forever without Christ, them two, had God not turned Brother Jim into a real ambassador. Some preachers now just up and talk so loud a body can't hear what they're saying. But not Brother Jim! He took the Scriptures literally—said 'twas like Paul told them Ephesians. The Good Book was a *sword* used by the Holy Spirit.

How? Well now, children, Brother Jim never owned no old-time sword. Didn't need one. His tongue was honed sharp as a straight razor! *Sure* they remembered the exact words! How could anybody forget such powerful witnessing?

"You promised, preacher—said you'd protect me iffen I confessed—"

"I promised no such thing, Lum—not to you or Josiah. I've got no power on my own. It's the Almighty who's your salvation. And it strikes me that He don't take a shine to people who claim to have seen the light and go right on carousing. Just look at you two—you and that snake in the grass, Horace Bellevue. Hypocrites! Pretenders of piety! Why, you've not an ounce of repentance in your liquor-sopping hearts! Guess I really ought to turn you over to the law—" Brother Jim pretended to be thinking.

Both the transgressors dropped to their knees, pleading for another chance. "That's up to the Lord," Brother Jim said. "And you'd better be praying instead of sniveling! As for me, gentlemen, I'm willing to ask that you be released to my custody—now, now—before you go thanking me, you've a right to know it's no easy sentence. We're going to study. We're going to pray. Then, you're going to walk the straight and narrow, having confessed your sins openly before the congregation! Signs of your redemption will be the lives you live. Otherwise, you'd be a heap safer with the marshal than in the ring with me!"

* * *

Easter Sunday! All was in readiness for the wedding. Courtney, looking like a tulip in her scallop-skirted pink dress, asked for a moment alone with the ancestors.

In the library, she moved from one great-grandfather to the other to tell them that the awful conflict between the Bellevues and the Glamoras had ended. Surely, now they could rest in peace.

Grandfather Bellevue's pale good looks had faded in the portraits as had Mother's and Vanessa's in real life. Grandfather Glamora's skin tone had lost its dark austerity. Only the piercing eyes remained unchanged— staring as if to question the happiness of his descendants. She should have had Lance touch up the portraits, Courtney supposed. And then, with a characteristic lift of her chin, she looked into the kindly eyes of her father, "Big Gabe."

"No—no, I should leave them as they are, dear Father," she whispered. "We will let those before us fade into the background where they belong. And, with God's help, this I promise—I shall carry on in your tradition."

216

Turning away, with tears in her dark eyes, Courtney focused on Lance's painting, "Another Spring." Winter was a natural part of life, but its tears would forever be dried by another spring. It was not a perfect world, but . . .

Something from long ago reached out and touched her heart. A portion of Paul's letter to the Philippians which her father loved so much. How did it go? " 'I press toward the mark—," Courtney murmured, trying to remember the sequence of the verses. " 'Not as though I had already attained, either were already perfect—' "

Clint tiptoed in. "Not perfect—but we are perfect *halves!*"

From downstairs came the ring of children's laughter. And, above it, the unmistakable mating call of a wild pigeon, rejoicing in the miracle of spring.

Another resurrection was at hand. Therein lay love . . . eternal truth . . . and the promise of perfection.

HARVEST HOUSE PUBLISHERS
For The Best In Inspirational Fiction

RUTH LIVINGSTON HILL CLASSICS

Bright Conquest
The Homecoming
The Jeweled Sword

Morning Is For Joy
This Side of Tomorrow
The South Wind Blew Softly

June Masters Bacher
PIONEER ROMANCE NOVELS

Series 1

1 Love Is a Gentle Stranger
2 Love's Silent Song

3 Diary of a Loving Heart
4 Love Leads Home

Series 2

1 Journey To Love
2 Dreams Beyond Tomorrow

3 Seasons of Love
4 My Heart's Desire

Series 3

1 Love's Soft Whisper
2 Love's Beautiful Dream

3 When Hearts Awaken
4 Another Spring

MYSTERY/ROMANCE NOVELS

Echoes From the Past, *Bacher*
Mist Over Morro Bay, *Page/Fell*
Secret of the East Wind, *Page/Fell*
Storm Clouds Over Paradise, *Page/Fell*
Beyond the Windswept Sea, *Page/Fell*
The Legacy of Lillian Parker, *Holden*
The Compton Connection, *Holden*
The Caribbean Conspiracy, *Holden*
The Gift, *Hensley/Miller*

PIONEER ROMANCE NOVELS

Sweetbriar, *Wilbee*
The Sweetbriar Bride, *Wilbee*
The Tender Summer, *Johnson*

Available at your local Christian bookstore

Other Good
Harvest House Reading

LOVE'S SOFT WHISPER
by *June Masters Bacher*

In just seconds Courtney Glamora's world split in half. Her mother was sending her away again—and this time far away to the Columbia Territory. Now the shy 16-year-old finds herself caught in the center of a lingering family feud. Through a special relationship Courtney learns to trust God and uncovers long-hidden secrets.

LOVE'S BEAUTIFUL DREAM
by *June Masters Bacher*

In this anxiously awaited sequel to *Love's Soft Whisper*, Clint Desmond and Courtney Glamora deepen their relationship with the Lord and with each other as they face and overcome Clint's tragic accident, their broken engagement, and the fear and regret that threaten their life together.

WHEN HEARTS AWAKEN
by *June Masters Bacher*

Clint and Courtney's love triumphs at last in *When Hearts Awaken*, and they are married in a beautiful Christmas Eve wedding. But the ensuing days of deepening love are soon torn asunder by Courtney's struggle between the mother who tries to control her and her love for her husband, for whom she has pledged to "forsake all others."

But it is the mysterious secrets of Rambling Gate that pose a dangerous threat to Courtney and Clint. It is there that Courtney's world explodes, robbing her of the promise of motherhood.

In the face of growing sorrow and the widening gulf between herself and her beloved husband, Courtney must find renewed hope and the courage to once again believe in God's faithfulness.

Other Good
Harvest House Reading

QUIET MOMENTS FOR WOMEN
by *June Masters Bacher*

Though written for women, this devotional will benefit the entire family. Mrs. Bacher's down-to-earth, often humorous experiences have a daily message of God's love for you!

GOD'S BEST FOR MY LIFE
by *Lloyd John Ogilvie*

Not since Oswald Chambers' *My Utmost for His Highest* has there been such an inspirational yet easy-to-read devotional. Dr. Ogilvie provides guidelines for maximizing your prayer and meditation time.

THE GRACIOUS WOMAN
Developing a Servant's Heart Through Hospitality
by *June Curtis*

June shares the secret of being a gracious woman and shows how to become the gracious woman God intended.

Dear Reader:

We would appreciate hearing from you regarding the June Masters Bacher Love's Soft Whisper Series. It will enable us to continue to give you the best in inspirational romance fiction.

Mail to: Love's Soft Whisper Editors
Harvest House Publishers, 1075 Arrowsmith
Eugene, OR 97402

1. What most influenced you to purchase *ANOTHER SPRING*?
   - ☐ The Christian story
   - ☐ Cover
   - ☐ Backcover copy
   - ☐ _____
   - ☐ Recommendations
   - ☐ Other June Masters Bacher Pioneer Romances you've read

2. Where did you purchase *ANOTHER SPRING*?
   - ☐ Christian bookstore
   - ☐ General bookstore
   - ☐ Other
   - ☐ Grocery store
   - ☐ Department store

3. Your overall rating of this book:
   - ☐ Excellent ☐ Very good ☐ Good ☐ Fair ☐ Poor

4. How many Bacher Love's Soft Whisper Romances have you read altogether?
   (Choose one) ☐ 1 ☐ 2 ☐ 3 ☐ Over 3

5. How likely would you be to purchase other Bacher Love's Soft Whisper Romances?
   - ☐ Very likely
   - ☐ Somewhat likely
   - ☐ Not very likely
   - ☐ Not at all

6. Please check the box next to your age group.
   - ☐ Under 18
   - ☐ 18-24
   - ☐ 25-34
   - ☐ 35-39
   - ☐ 40-54
   - ☐ Over 55

Name _____

Address _____

City _____ State _____ Zip _____